See the Earth and Die!

"Very good," he said. *"Very good pictures."* Then his voice changed. *"See the Earth and then die."*

"I do not understand. . . ."

"It is an old saying that I just made up. Thanks for letting me see the pictures. They brought back memories."

It was not possible. But I had to ask him. "Just how old are you, Mr. Black?"

"There are too many ways to answer your question," he said. "But I see what you are really asking. Yes, I have seen the Earth—actually, not just in pictures. I remember what things were like, before the House was built."

"No," I said. "That is physically impossible."

"Perhaps you are right, Lange," he said.

"How is it that you know my name?" I asked him.

Reaching into his pocket, he said, "I owe you something."

"See the Earth," he said, and, "Arrivederci!"

I felt the bullet enter my heart. . . .

SIGNET Science Fiction You Will Enjoy

Today
We Choose Faces

by ROGER ZELAZNY

A SIGNET BOOK from
NEW AMERICAN LIBRARY
TIMES MIRROR

FIRST PRINTING
SECOND PRINTING
THIRD PRINTING
FOURTH PRINTING
FIFTH PRINTING
SIXTH PRINTING
SEVENTH PRINTING
EIGHTH PRINTING
NINTH PRINTING
TENTH PRINTING

 SIGNET TRADEMARK REG. U.S. PAT. OFF. AND FOREIGN COUNTRIES
REGISTERED TRADEMARK—MARCA REGISTRADA
HECHO EN CHICAGO, U.S.A.

SIGNET, SIGNET CLASSICS, SIGNETTE, MENTOR AND PLUME BOOKS
are published by The New American Library, Inc.,
1301 Avenue of the Americas, New York, New York 10019

FIRST PRINTING, APRIL, 1973

PRINTED IN THE UNITED STATES OF AMERICA

To Philip K. Dick,
electric shepherd

Part I

Drifting . . . Placid, yet relentless. Peaceful, yet merciless. Drifting.

A bolt of lightning, followed by an infinite sigh . . .

Rushing, falling . . .

A slow shower of jigsaw pieces, some of them coming together about me . . .

. . . And I began to know.

It was as if I had known all along, though.

Then the picture was complete, and I beheld it in its entirety as from a timeless vantage.

There was a sequence, of course, like vertebrae or dominoes, and it was not at all difficult to here, here, there it.

Here. For example.

. . . Leaving the club on a cold Saturday night in November. A little after 10:30, I guess. Eddie was with me, and we stood behind the glass doors at the front of the place, buttoning our overcoats and looking out at a damp Manhattan street, gusts of wind sailing bits of paper past us, while we waited for Denny to bring the car around. We said nothing. He knew I was still in a bad temper. I took out a cigarette. He hurried to light it for me.

Finally, the glossy black sedan drew up. I had just pulled one glove on and was holding the other. Eddie moved forward and opened the door, held it for me. I stepped outside and the chill air stung my eyes, bringing tears to them. I paused to get out a handkerchief and wipe them, mainly conscious then of the wind, the idling of the engine and a few distant horn notes.

As I lowered the handkerchief I became immediately aware of another figure which had appeared in the car, in the rear seat, and in the same instant realized that the rear window was down and that Eddie had moved six or seven paces away from me.

I heard some of the gunfire, felt the impact of a couple of the slugs. It was to be a long while before I learned that I had been hit four times.

My only consolation right before the lights went out was, twisting as I fell, seeing the smile vanish from Eddie's face, his hand jerking after, but not making it to his own weapon, and then the slow beginning of his topple.

And that was the last I ever saw of him, falling, an instant before he hit the pavement.

Here. For another.

Listening to Paul talk, I regarded what could have been a lovely view of a bright mountain lake fed by a little stream, a giant willow tree quivering beside it as if chilled by the water it tested with the green and shiny tips of its limbs. It was a fake. That is, it was real, but the picture was relayed from a spot hundreds of miles away. It was more pleasant than looking out a window from his upper-floor apartment, though, when all I could see would be a section—albeit a neat, attractive area—of that urban complex which extended from New York to Washington. The suite was soundproof, air-conditioned and I suppose tastefully decorated in accordance with the best sensibility of the times. I could not judge, since I was not yet familiar with the times. Its brandy was excellent, though.

". . . Must have been puzzling as all hell," Paul was saying. "I am amazed at how quickly you have adapted."

I turned and looked at him again, a slim, still-young, dark-haired man with an engaging smile and eyes that really told nothing of what went on behind. He was still a thing of fascination for me. My grandson, with six or seven greats in front of the word. I kept looking for resemblances, finding them where least expected. The jut of the brow, the short upper lip, heavy lower one. The nose was his own, but then he had our way of quirking the left corner of his mouth at moments of pique or amusement.

I sent the smile back.

"Nothing that amazing about it," I replied. "The fact that I made the provisions I did should have indicated I had done some thinking about the future."

"I guess so," he said. "But to tell the truth, my only

thought was that you had been looking for an out on death."

"Of course I was. I was aware of the possibility of my getting it the way that I did, and while body-freezing was still a fairly novel thing back in the 'seventies—"

"The *nineteen*-seventies," he interrupted, with another smile.

"Yes, I do make it sound like just a couple of years ago, don't I? Try it sometime and you will understand the feeling. Anyway, I figured what the hell. If I got shot down, whatever got damaged might be replaceable— someday. Why not set things up to have them freeze me and hope for the best? I had read a few articles on the subject, and it sounded like it might work. So I did. After that, it was funny . . . It got to be kind of an obsession with me. I mean, I got to thinking about it quite a bit, the way a real religious man might think about heaven—like, 'When I die, I'll go to the future.' Then I found myself wondering more and more what it would be like. I did a lot of thinking and a lot of reading, trying to figure different ways that things might work out. It wasn't a bad hobby," I said, taking another drink. "It gave me a lot of fun, and as things turned out it's paying off."

"Yes," he said. "So you were not really surprised to learn that a means of traveling faster than light was developed, and that we have visited worlds beyond the solar system?"

"Of course I was surprised. But I had been hoping for it."

"And the recent successes in teleportation, on an interstellar scale?"

"I was more surprised at that. Pleasantly, though. Hooking the outposts together that way will be a great achievement."

"Then let me ask you what you have found the most surprising."

"Well," I said, finding myself a seat and taking another sip, "outside of the fact that we managed to get this far and still have not found a way to remove the possibility of war—" I raised a hand at this point as he began to interrupt me with something about controls and sanctions. He shut up. I was glad to see that he respected his elders. "Outside of that," I went on, "I suppose that the single

11

most surprising thing to me is that we have gone more or less legitimate."

He grinned.

"What do you mean 'more or less'?"

I shrugged.

"Well?" I said.

"We are as legitimate as anybody," he countered, "or we would never have been able to get listed on the World Stock Exchange."

I said nothing, but found another smile.

"Of course, it is a very well-run organization."

"I would be disappointed if it were not."

"Just so, just so," he said. "But there we are. COSA Inc. All legal, proper and respectable. Been that way for generations. The tendency in that direction had actually begun in your day, with—as feature writers liked to put it—the 'laundering' of funds and their reinvestment in more acceptable enterprises. Why fight the system when you are strong enough to be big in it without fighting? What are a few dollars one way or the other when you can have everything you want and security, too? Without the risks. Just by following the rules."

"All of them?"

"Well, there are so many that it has become, if anything, easier, when you can afford the brainpower."

He finished his drink, fetched us refills.

"There is no stigma," he concluded then. "The image we had in your day is ancient history now."

He leaned forward conspiratorily.

"It must really have been something, though, living in those times," he said, and then he looked at me expectantly.

I did not know whether to be irritated or flattered. From the way they had been treating me since my arousal a couple of weeks earlier, I obviously shared some historical niche with the bedpan and the brontosaurus. On the other hand, Paul seemed to regard me with more than a little pride, rather like a family heirloom which had been entrusted to his keeping. By then, I was aware that his position in the organization's power structure was both secure and potent. He had insisted that I be his houseguest, though I could have been put up elsewhere. He seemed to take a great delight in getting me to talk

12

about my life and times. I learned slowly that his knowledge of these things was largely based on the gaudier writings, films and rumors of the day. Still, I was eating his food, sleeping under his roof, we were relatives and the statutes had long since run. So I obliged him with some reminiscences.

It might have disappointed him that I had spent a couple of years in college before taking over my father's business when he met his sudden, untimely end, but the fact that I spent a chunk of my earliest life in Sicily before he had sent for the family seemed to make up for this. Then I believe I disappointed him again when I told him that to the best of my knowledge there had never been a worldwide criminal conspiracy centered there. I saw the *onorata società* as a local, not unbeneficial, family-centered thing, which had in its time produced such notable *galantuomi* as Don Vito Cascio Ferro and Don Calò Vizzini. I tried to explain that there was a necessary distinction between the *società degli amici* with its own, parochial interests and individuals who migrated, who may or may not have been *amici*, who engaged in illicit activities and preferred doing business with one another rather than with strangers, and who preserved a strong family tradition. Paul was as much a victim of the conspiracy mystique as any tabloid devourer, however, and was convinced I was still preserving some secret tradition or other. I gradually came to see that he was something of a romantic, that he wanted things to have been the other way, that he wanted to be part of the unreal tradition. So I told him some of the things I knew he would enjoy hearing.

I told him how I had dealt with the matter of my father's passing, as well as several other encounters which helped justify my name, Angelo di Negri. Somewhere along the line, the family had later changed it to Nero. Not that that mattered to me. I was who I was. And Paul Nero smiled and nodded and lapped up the details. He had an infinite capacity for secondhand violence.

All of which may sound somewhat contemptuous, but is not, not really. For I came to like him considerably as time went on. Perhaps this was because he reminded me somewhat of myself, in another time and place—a softer, easier-going, more urbane version. Perhaps he was like

13

something that I might have been, or wished that I could have afforded the luxury of trying to be.

But I was pushing forty. My character had long ago hardened. Though the circumstances that shaped me had long since passed, my pleasures in a, to me, almost pressureless society, were infiltrated by notes scored to a different measure, resulting at first in a vague uneasiness, to be followed by a growing dissatisfaction. Life is seldom so pivotally crisis-conditioned a thing as novelists would have us believe. While it is true that we sometimes recover from shocks with a sense of the freshness of reality and the wonder of existence, this state of mind does pass away—and fairly rapidly, at that—leaving both reality and ourselves untransfigured once more. Consciousness of this fact came to me as I sat sentimentalizing past crudities for my descendant, and grew into a major discontent during the weeks that followed. I had not changed much, though everything else had. It was not completely a sense of being superfluous, though there was something of that, nor could it be nostalgia, as my memories were sufficiently recent and substantial to preclude any glossing over of what, to Paul, was the distant past. Perhaps it was a growing sensitivity to the fact that people seemed a trifle gentler, more pacific, that aroused some feelings of inferiority, as though I had just missed out on some necessary step in the process of civilization. I was not ordinarily given to such introspection, but when feelings become sufficiently strong and persistent they force their own exploration.

Still, how does one picture his mental life to anyone, let alone one who seems a distorted image of himself? What I wanted to say was manifold and not the sort of thing that could really be communicated by words.

Paul may have done better than I thought in understanding it, in understanding me, though. For he made two suggestions, one of which I followed immediately, while thinking about the other.

There. For example.

I went back to Sicily. An almost predictable thing, I would say, for a man in my circumstances and state of mind. Aside from the obvious associations it held, reaching back to my childhood, I had learned that it was one of the remaining places in the world which had not yet suffered

14

from overdevelopment. It was then, in a very real way, a means of traveling back through time for me.

I did not stay long in Palermo, but headed almost immediately into the hinterland. I rented an isolated place that had a familiar feeling to it, and spent several hours every day riding one of the two horses that had come with it. Mornings, I would ride down to the rocky shore and watch the surf come creaming and booming toward me, picking my way along the wet shingles it slid from, listening to the squawks of the birds as they arced and dipped above it, breathing the acrid sea-wind, watching the play of dazzle and shade across the graywhitebleak prospect. Afternoons or evenings, as the mood moved me, I would often ride in the hills, where scraggly grass and twisted trees clung desperately to the thin soil and the damp breath of the Mediterranean drifted sultry or cool, as the mood moved it, about me. If I did not stare too long at the several stationary stars, if I did not raise my eyes when a transport vehicle flashed high and fast over head, if I refrained from using the communications unit for anything but music and rode to the nearest small town but once every week or so for perishable supplies, it was almost as though no time at all had passed for me. Not just the intervening century, but my entire adult life seemed to recede and fade into the timeless landscape of my youth. So what happened then was not wholly inexplicable.

Her name was Julia, and I encountered her for the first time in a rocky cul-de-sac that grew lush by comparison with the bruise-colored hills through which I had been riding all that afternoon. She was seated on the ground beneath a tree which resembled a frozen fountain of marmalade to which some pale confetti had adhered, her dark hair drawn back and fastened with a coral clip, sketchpad in her lap, eyes darting and hand shifting, precise, deliberate, as she sketched a small flock of sheep. For a time, I just sat there and watched her, but then a cloud moved on and the emerging sun cast my long shadow down past her.

She turned then, and shaded her eyes. I dismounted, twisted the reins about a nearby shrub's handiest branch and headed down.

"Hello," I said, as I approached.

15

It was ten or fifteen seconds before I reached her, and it took her that long to decide to nod and smile slightly.

"Hello," she said.

"My name's Angelo. I was riding by and saw you, saw this place—thought it might be pleasant to stop and smoke a cigarette, to watch you draw. If that's all right?"

She nodded, bit into the lower half of a new smile, accepted a cigarette.

"I'm Julia," she said. "I work here."

"Artist in residence?"

"Bio-tech. This is just a hobby," she said, tapping the pad and letting her hand remain to cover her work.

"Oh? What are you bioteching?"

She nodded toward the woolly crowd.

"Her," she said.

"Which one is she?"

"All of them."

"I'm afraid I don't follow . . ."

"They are clones," she said, "each one grown from the tissue of a single donor."

"Neat trick, that," I said. "Tell me about clones," and I seated myself on the grass and watched it being eaten.

She seemed to welcome the opportunity to close the pad without letting me see her work. She launched into the story of her flock, and it required only a few questions here and there for me to learn somewhat of herself also.

She was originally from Catania, but she had been to school in France and was presently in the employ of an institute in Switzerland which was doing research in animal husbandry and was employing cloning techniques to field-test promising specimens in various environments simultaneously. She was twenty-six and had just ended a marriage on a very sour note and gotten herself transferred to the field with a test flock. She had been back in Sicily for a little over two months. She told me a lot about clones, really warming to the subject in the face of my obvious ignorance, describing in overabundant detail the processes whereby her sheep had been grown from cellular specimens of a hybrid in Switzerland to replicate her in all details. She even told me of the peculiar and still not understood resonance effect, which involved the fact that all of them would exhibit temporary symptoms of the same illness should one of them be stricken—in-

16

cluding the original in Switzerland and others in other parts of the world. No, to the best of her knowledge, cloning had not yet been attempted at the level of human beings—myriad legal, scientific and religious objections existed—although there were rumors concerning experimentation on one of the outpost worlds. While she apparently knew her business quite well, it struck me after a time that her words were put forth more with a pleasure at having someone to talk to than from any desire too inform. And we had this, too, in common.

But I did not tell her my own story that day. I listened, we sat a time in silence, watching the sheep, watching the lengthening shadows, talked again, in a desultory fashion, of small, neutral matters. As we talked, a mutual assumption gradually became manifest in our speech, that this was but a part of a continuing conversation, that I would be back, the next day or the day after, that we would be seeing one another again, and again. Nor was this assumption incorrect.

Before very long, she became interested in horseback riding. Soon we were riding together every day, mornings or evenings, sometimes both. I told her where I was from, and how, omitting only what I had done there and the exact nature of my passing. I did not realize that I was falling in love until long after we had become lovers. I did not discover the fact until the day I determined to reach a decision on Paul's second suggestion and I realized how much of a factor she had become in my thinking.

I rose, crossed the room to the window, drew back the curtain, stared up through the night. The embers in the grate still glowed cherry and orange. The outer cold had passed through the walls and was pressing now like a spiritual glacier toward our corner of the room.

"I must be leaving soon," I said.

"Where will you go?"

"I may not say."

Silence. Then, "Will you be coming back?"

I had no answer, though I wished I did.

"Would you like me to?"

Silence again. Then, "Yes."

"I will try to," I said.

Why was I going to take the Styler contract? I had

17

wanted to from the moment Paul had described the situation to me. A high-level sinecure with the company and a big block of expensive stock were but the surface returns on the thing. I had no illusion that my thawing, my treatment, my recovery had been the result of an unsullied desire for my company on the part of my descendants. The necessary techniques had been available for several decades. It is not unpleasant to feel needed, however, no matter what the reasons. My pleasure at their attentiveness was in no way vitiated by the knowledge that I had something they wanted. If anything, it was enhanced. What other hold had I on the day? I was more than just a curiosity. I had a value that went beyond the emotions of the moment, and its realization could restore to me some measure of mastery, could earn me another sort of appreciation. I had been thinking about this, or something like it, earlier when I had drawn rein above the nearest village at a place where the olive terraces rose to scrub and bleakness, and stared down at the light and movement. Shortly, Julia came up beside me.

"What is it?" she had asked.

I was wondering at that moment what it would have been like if I had awakened with no memories of my earlier existence. Would it have made it easier or more difficult to find me some slot in life, to be satisfied with it? Might I then be like the inhabitants of the village below, bringing interest and something of pleasure to simple actions at their ten thousandth repetition?

Standing beside a shallow, sheltered inlet on a warm, bright afternoon, watching the reflected ripple of the water trace trembling lines across her naked breasts as she stopped splashing and the smile went out of her face and she said, "What is it?" I was thinking of the seventeen men I had killed back when they had begun calling me "Angie the Angel," as I had risen through the ranks to secure that earlier existence. Paul had not known about all of the killings, of course. I was surprised that he had known of as many as he did—eight, to be exact, the names spoken with a measure of confidence I did not feel he could have faked. For my part, I found it virtually inconceivable that the legal niceties and organization-chart formalities had become something more than a facade, that in fact there were few reliable professional

18

killers to be had any more. So it seemed that I had indeed brought something of value across the years with me. I had for the most part personally eschewed such activities, however, once I had secured my position at a higher level within the organization. Now, to be offered a contract, in a sedate time of almost total cultural availability, smoothly meshing gears, life prolongation and interstellar travel . . . It seemed more than a little strange, no matter how delicately Paul put it.

As we had eaten oranges in the shade of the water-processing plant, its doubtless onetime sleek and shiny walls softened partly by weather and partly by the intervention of lilac and wisteria to a monastery-like finish, I had stroked her hair and she had plucked the pale-green hellebore, that ancient remedy for madness, tangling those flowers in my own, and my thoughts had strayed beyond the severely drawn diagrams of skull and walls, softened by their froths of blossoms, and into the completely automatic workings of the installation, whose sounds were repeated to us, softly, inevitably, as it took in, purified and spewed through underground conduits I knew not how many thousands of gallons of the sea, and I considered the dual nature of Herbert Styler, field representative for Doxford Industries on the planet called Alvo, so far removed from the pale human star we formed as to be equally inconceivable, but this time she did not notice and say, "What is it?" as I wondered whether the man who had undergone experimental neural abridgment of a kind still illegal on Earth, supposedly permitting him full conscious access to the workings of a great computer complex, whether this man, who, for his company, stood in the way of COSA's expansion on the choicest of the outworlds, could be considered a machine with a human personality or a man with a computer mind, and whether what I had been asked to do was properly homicide or something totally new—say, mechanicide or cybicide—while the muted thudding of the sea and the nearer vibration of the waterworks came into us, along with the fragrances of the blossoms and the touch of salt the breezes bore.

Paul had assured me that I would be given the best training and equipment available for the fulfillment of the contract. He had then recommended that I take a trip.

"Get away for a time," he had said, and, "Think about it."

Staring up through the night, feeling the cold, wondering whether I could kill him, get away, come back and start over, fresh and clean, belonging here, my other life as dead and sealed then ...

"I will try to," I said, and let the curtain fall.

Here, then.

... Seeing her seated beneath that crazy holiday-tree, soft hair fixed with a pale, coral clip, head and hand moving as she transferred her sheep to paper, precise, deliberate; then a brightening of the day, the fall of my shadow, her attention, the turning of her head, the movement of her arm as she raised her hand to shade her eyes, me dismounting, twisting the reins about a branch, starting down toward her, reaching for a word, a face, her nod, her slow smile ...

Here.

... Seeing the fire-flowers unfold all in a row beneath me, the final blossom covering half of the building, its target; my vehicle faltering, diving, burning then, myself ejected, the cabin intact about me and moving with a life of its own, dodging, darting, firing, downward and forward, downward and forward, coming apart then and dropping me gently, gently down, my prosthetic armor making the barest of clicks as my feet touch the ground and the repellors cut off; and then my lasers lancing forward, cutting through the figures who advance upon me, grenades flying from my hands, waves of protoplasm-shattering ultrasonics flowing from me like notes from some rung, invisible bell ...

How many androids and robots I smashed, mockup buildings I razed, obstacles I destroyed, projectiles I hurled in the two months that followed, there on that barren worldlet where I was taken to be familiarized with all the latest methods of violence, I do not know. Many. My instructors were technicians, not killers, who would later undergo memory-erasure, to protect both the organization and themselves. The discovery that this was possible intrigued me, recalling to me some of my earlier thoughts. The techniques, I learned, were highly sophisticated and could be employed quite selectively. They had been in use for years as a psychotherapeutic tool. The instructors, for their part, were a strange mixture of attitudes and moods, at first exhorting me almost constantly to perfect my techniques with their weapons while scrupulously avoiding any reference to the fact that I would soon be using them to kill someone. Later, however, as the realization gathered that whatever they said or felt or thought would subsequently be removed from their consciousness, they began to joke frequently about death and killing and their feelings toward me seemed to undergo a reversal. From an initial state of undisguised contempt, they came in a matter of weeks to regard me with something approaching reverence, as if I were a sort of priest and they vicarious participants in a sacrifice. This disturbed me, and I took to avoiding them as much as possible on my own time. For me, the job was simply something that I had to do, to find my place in what seemed a better society than the one I had left. It was then that I began to wonder whether people were changing rapidly enough to assure the race's continued existence, if these men could revert so readily, reach so eagerly for a violence-fix. I had few illusions concerning myself, and I was willing to try to live with me for the rest of my life; but I had considered them my moral superiors, and it was their society I was trying to buy into. It was not until near the end of my training, however, that I learned something of the dynamics which underlay their altered attitude. Hanmer, one of the least objectionable of my instructors, came to my quarters one night, bearing a bottle which made him somewhat welcome. He had already done considerable work on its predecessor, and his face, which normally bore the certainty of expression generally found only on ventriloquists' dummies, had grown rather slack, his voice slowed from its usual chatter to a thing of slow puzzlement. It was not long before I learned what was bothering him. The sanctions and controls were not doing so well. It appeared that a limited armed conflict—the situation to which I had alluded when speaking with Paul some time before—had moved several steps nearer actuality, was indeed imminent, as Hanmer saw it. The politics of it bored me, for they were not yet mine, but the possibility of its occurring at all, with the ever-present danger of its growing into something large and terrifying, was ironic as well as

21

alarming. To come all this way, and in the manner that I did, just to arrive in time for a worldwide conflagration ... No! It was absurd. Absolutely. It began to seem that their proximity to an instrument of violence, myself, at a time like this had served to trigger something quite deep-seated and well suppressed within these men. While it had released something violent and irrational within the others, in the case of Hanmer, who, after a time, sat monotonously repeating, "It can't happen," it had broken something.

"It may not," I said, to hearten him, since it was his whisky I was drinking.

He looked at me then. Hope seemed to flicker for a moment, then went away from his eyes.

"What do you care?" he said.

"I care. It's my world, too. Now."

He looked away.

"I don't understand you," he said at last. "Or the others, for that matter ..."

I thought that I did, though it was of small help to anybody. All my emotions at the moment were things based on absence.

I waited. I did not know him well enough to know why his reaction should be different from the others', and I never did find out. He said one other thing that remained with me, though.

"... But I think everybody ought to be locked up till they learn how to behave."

Trite, laughable and quite impossible, of course. At the time.

Mixing the remainder of the booze into two stiff ones, I hastened him on his way to oblivion, partly regretting there was not a bit more around, so that I might follow him.

Here, here, and then: There ...

[Stars]	[Out of the tunnel under the sky & down]

22

[Entry]	.	[Strobe lights
	.	& thunder]
	.	
	.	
	.	
	.	
	.	[Song of the air]
[Clouds	.	[Invisible fingers
	.	of matter]
	.	
	.	
	.	
clouds	.	
	.	
	.	
cl ou d s]	.	
	.	
	.	
[Explosion #1]	.	[Lasciate ogni
[#2] [#3]	.	sper- anza
	.	voi ch'
	.	en- trate?]
	.	
	.	

. . . were flashes like scissors of lightning cutting the sky apart. Despite the shielding and my distance from the detonations, I was batted about like a shuttlecock. I was hunched forward in my battle armor, letting the computer deal with these disturbances, but ready to cut in on manual should the need arise. Alvo flashed beneath me in a too-quick pattern of greenbrown-grayblue for me to distinguish features, unless perhaps I had had the time to simply sit and stare down at it. But I was not especially tense as I wound the miles inside me, annihilating the distance, threading its thunder. To do the job as quickly as was deemed necessary now allowed no time for subtlety. Doxford's internal security setup was too strong for anything short of a years-long infiltration campaign. A surprise thrust, a juggernaut attack, had therefore been decided upon as having the best possibility for success. Styler's defense was excellent, but we had expected nothing less.

He must have picked me up almost immediately upon my appearance in the vicinity of Alvo. I spent little time wondering at the technical feat involved in my detection, as I swept along, low now, speeding toward that fortress of an office complex where he made his headquarters, but I wondered what Styler's thoughts and feelings must have been when first he had noted me. How long had he expected this attack? How much might he know concerning it?

For a time then, I dodged or withstood everything he threw at me, my own weapons systems ready to come into play in an instant. I hoped to at least commence my assault from the air.

A crackle of static, a whistle, a sound of heavy breathing. My radio had come to life. I had not expected this. It seemed something of an exercise in futility for anyone to try to threaten or cajole me at this point.

However, "Unidentified vessel and etcetera, you are passing over unauthorized such-and-such. You are ordered to . . ." did not emerge.

Instead, "Angie the Angel," I heard. "Welcome to Alvo. Are you finding your brief visit interesting?"

So he knew who I was. And it was Styler himself speaking. I had heard his voice and viewed his likeness many times in the course of my preparations. I had had to force my instructors to cut a programmed accompaniment of vilification which had been part of the familiarization sessions, as I had found it distracting. They found it difficult to believe that I did not feel it necessary to hate the short, pale-eyed man with the puffy cheeks and the turban about his head that covered the terminals of his permanent implants. "Of course it is propaganda," they said, "but it will help you when the time comes." I shook my head slowly. "I do not need emotions to help me kill," I told them. "They might even get in the way." They had to accept this, but it was plain that they did not understand.

24

So he knew who I was. It was surprising, but hardly prostrating. Tremendous amounts of current information were regularly dumped into his computer adjunct, and he was supposedly possessed of a sound, somewhat spectacular mind, complete with imagination. So while I felt he was guessing, it was doubtless a very informed guess, and of course an accurate one. I saw no reason to talk with him, though; or, for that matter, not to talk with him. It made no difference at all to me. Words could change nothing.

Still, "It *will* be a brief visit," he insisted. "You will not be leaving here, you know."

A shaft of something like lightning ran through a dark cloud, ahead/beside/behind me. The ship shook, some circuits sputtered, a wave of static took away some of Styler's words.

".. are not the first," he said. "Obviously, none of the others ..."

Others? He could have tossed that out just hoping to upset me. But it was something I had not considered. Paul had never said that I was the first to attempt this. In fact, thinking about it, it was probable that I was not. While this did not disturb me, I did wonder how many others there might have been.

No matter. Contemporary kids. They had probably required the brainwashing business, had needed to work up a hatred in order to essay the thing. Their business. Their funerals. It was not my way.

"You can still call it off, Angel," he said. "Land your vessel and remain with it. I will send someone to pick you up. You will live. What do you say?"

I chuckled. He must have heard it, because, "At least I know you are there," he said. "Your attack is an exercise in futility in more ways than one. Outside of the fact that you have no chance of succeeding and will doubtless die here, and soon, the reasons for your making the effort at all have been removed."

He paused then, as if waiting for me to say something. That was his exercise in futility.

"Not interested, eh?" he said then. "Any moment now my defensive assault will pierce your screen. COSA had no way of knowing what I have added to the system since their previous effort. Any one of these next might do it."

25

There followed a series of jarring explosions. I emerged from these without mishap, however.

"Still there," he observed. "Good. That still allows you a chance to change your mind. I would like you to live, you know, as I should be very interested in talking with a man like you, from another time, a man with your background. As I began to say, there are other reasons than fatal obstacles for giving the thing up. I do not know what you may or may not have heard, because I know you have been offworld for a time, but it is true that there has been a war—and I suppose, technically, it is still in progress. From all reports I have received, the Earth is in a pretty sorry state just now. Both of our employers have been very hard-hit. In fact, I believe we lack home offices at the moment. This being the case, I see more need for salvaging whatever remains of both organizations than for continuing our conflict. What do you say?"

Of course I said nothing. I had no way to verify any of his talk, and he had no way of proving it to me, unless I were willing to land and take a look at whatever he might have to offer in the way of evidence—which was naturally out of the question. So there was no basis for conversation on that count.

I heard him sigh, across a tiny rivulet of static.

"You are determined that there be more death," he said then. "You think that everything I have told you is purely self-serving in nature . . ."

I almost cut him off then, because I do not like people who tell me what I am thinking, whether or not they are right. Still, it was the best show in town . . .

"Why don't you say something?" he said. "I would like to hear your voice. Tell me why you are about this business. If it is only money, I will pay you more to give it up—whatever they are paying you—and protect you afterward." He paused, waited, then went on, "Of course, with you, there is probably something else involved, too. Family loyalty. Solidarity. The tribal blood-bond. That sort of thing. If that is what it is, I will tell you something. You are probably the only one around who believes in it the old way any more. They do not. I know these men, have known them well for years, whereas you have only known them for a brief while. It is true. Their values are no longer yours. They are capitalizing on your loyalty.

26

They are using you. *Are* you doing it out of family loyalty? Is that what it is?"

His voice had sounded a bit strained near the end there. It was more relaxed when he started in again.

"It is a bit frustrating, talking to you this way," he said, "knowing you are out there, coming closer and closer by the moment—hearing me. Still, I see it your way now. You are determined. Nothing that I can say can change your mind. I can only try to kill you before you kill me. You are moving and I am fixed at this location. It is too late for me to try to flee. You will not succeed, of course. But, as I said, I see it your way now. You have nothing to say to me, and I really have nothing to say to you. This is what irritates me. You are not like the others. They all talked, you know. They threatened me, they cursed me, they died screaming. You are an ignorant barbarian, incapable of understanding what I am, but this does not deter you, does not disturb you. Does it? I was attempting something intended to benefit the entire human race, but this does not bother you. Does it? You simply remain silent and keep coming. Have you ever read Pascal? No. Of course you haven't ... 'Man is but a reed, the most feeble thing in nature,' he said, 'but he is a thinking reed. The entire universe need not arm itself to crush him. A vapor, a drop of water, suffices to kill him. But if the universe were to crush him, man would still be more noble than that which killed him, because he knows that he dies and the advantage which the universe has over him; the universe knows nothing of this.' Do you understand what I am saying? No, of course not. You never think of these matters. You are a vapor, a drop of water ... There comes a time, if there is some sort of fulfillment in life, when one can accept death, I believe, without too much in the way of resentment. I have not yet achieved such a state, but I have been working on it. Let me tell you—"

At that moment, the barrage rose to a sudden pitch of fierceness that lit up the sky, drowned all lesser sounds and hit me with shock waves that came like a maniac surf.

But then my target rocked into view, the Doxford Building, backed against the hills at the far end of a distant valley.

Moments later, I began the attack. Fountains of light

27

erupted from the floor of the valley and on the hillside. The right corner of the building crumbled, there was fire on the roof ...

I was hit myself, within instants of that small triumph, and immediately began the downward tumble. As I had not been ejected, I realized that the control section must be reasonably intact. A quick survey—physical, and via the warning-board—showed me that this was so. There had been a successful separation, though, and I caught glimpses of the twisted outer framework of the vessel plunging groundward.

Another hit, and while my armor would probably save me, I would be ejected. If I could make it to the ground with the cabin intact, though ...

"Are you still alive?" I heard Styler saying. "I see a piece—"

There came an explosion that took my attention away from his words, shaking, jolting, tumbling me about. I had the controls on manual by then, for I did not want to slow my descent until the last possible moment.

"Angel? Are you still there?"

I managed to convert all the necessary systems as I fell, braked at the last possible instant, hit at a bad angle, rolled, stabilized, brought the vehicle around intact. I slapped it into gear and rolled forward immediately after that.

I was at the opposite end of the still-smoking, dust-misted valley from the Doxford complex. It was quite rocky, and full of craters and potholes, not all of them recently formed. This seemed to lend some credibility to the assertion that mine was not the first attack on the place. It also made it difficult for the defenders to mine the area, a fact that came in handy as I proceeded through it, looking for potential boobytraps.

I could not help wondering whether he had spoken the truth about the war, though. My few tenuous links with the past and my only important ones with the present were all involved. I could see no reason for anyone bombing Sicily, though. But was she still there? Several months had passed, and people were very mobile these days. And how was Paul? And some of the others I had met? I knew they possessed elaborate shelters. Still ...

"You *are* alive! I've got you on the screens. Good! This

makes it even easier for you to throw in your hand. No worry about landing on a mine once you are already down. Listen. All you have to do is stop and wait now. I will send someone to pick you up. I will show you evidence to support everything I have said. What do you say?"

I eased my guns forward in their mounts, and swung them, elevated them, lowered them, to test the mountings.

"That, I take it, is your answer?" he said. "Look, it will gain you absolutely nothing to die here—and that is exactly what will happen. Our employers are both out of business by now. Your range is being taken even now, and you will shortly be blown to bits. It is senseless. Life is a precious thing, and so much of it has just vanished recently. The human race has just been more than decimated, and that remainder may well be reduced to a tenth also, from the lingering effects of this thing. Then there are the present difficulties facing the qualified remainder—rounding up the survivors and providing for them, rigging sufficient teleportation gates, transporting them offworld, trying to resettle them. The Earth is barely habitable, and conditions will continue to worsen. Most of the outworlds are not ready for prolonged human habitation, and we are in no position to change them further at the moment. Some sort of shelters have to be set up, communications established and maintained among the worlds. There is no need for more deaths, and I am offering you a chance to live. Can you accept that? Do you believe me?"

I achieved a fairly level run of rock and increased my speed. Through the smoke, the dust, the fumes, I could see that flames flickered behind the hole I had knocked in his fortress. No matter how certain he tried to sound as to his ability to destroy me, he could not gainsay the fact that I had scored a hit.

From somewhere at his end of the valley, the firing began—first short, then long, taking my measure. I varied my speeds, was thankful when I reached an irregular incline and started up it, for the angle seemed to throw them off a bit. I readied my rockets, though I hoped I could get in closer before firing them. I checked the time, sighed. It was past the time for arrival and detonation of the two high-powered missiles that had separated from the

29

flier the same time I had and gone on ahead. He had gotten them, then. Their chances had not really been that good, though.

Then the barrage began, shaking me, jarring me, bouncing me about. The noise became deafening, the flashes near-blinding, the smoke heavy. The ground vibrated, and fragments of rock were blasted against the vehicle, fell upon it in an almost steady hail.

"Hello? Hello?" I heard faintly within the noise. Then whatever followed was drowned out by three that came very close.

I swerved sharply, moved at an angle, straightened, utilizing the cover afforded by several high stands of stone. The firing became more erratic, falling farther and farther away from me. My radio had gone dead once I had gotten in behind the rocky hedge. I kept advancing, spotted a tricky and roundabout way leading off to my left and took it because it seemed somewhat sheltered. It did seem to baffle his detection, because his shots kept landing farther and farther afield.

As I worked my twisted way along, I almost overlooked another complex of buildings, deep in a coomb, still farther to my left. They were very new and seemed completely deserted. They had not been mentioned in my orientation, had not been indicated on any of the maps or photos I had studied. I kept them covered until I had passed, but had no reason to fire.

As I climbed higher, the radio found his voice again, faintly at first, strengthening as I went.

". . . So you see," he was saying, "I am free for the first time in my life, free to use some of these things I have developed as they should be used—noncommercially, for the benefit of the entire race—to help get us through these perilous times. There is a great need for my abilities, my facilities, now. Even the cloning tech—"

I had been spotted. A series of heavy explosions occurred behind me. Moments later, I had rounded my sheltering rocks and was out in the open once more. There was scant cover for hundreds of yards, and the way was entirely uphill. I moved forward with all the speed I possessed, knowing that my luck had just about run and hoping that it would hold a few moments more so that I could fire my rockets. From the position I then occupied, it would be virtually impossible to reach him.

The next ones landed far ahead of me, and I swerved to avoid the blasted area. Moments later, there was another to the rear, very close this time.

But I made it to my shelter, spent a handful of heartbeats working in close and toward the right while the rocks were pounded and splintered ahead of me, then ventured a diagonal dash toward another, nearer refuge.

I did not deserve to make it, and I almost didn't. I was hit seconds after I pulled out, and I spun completely around. I was lifted off the ground, dropped, bounced and given a sudden, unexpected view of the shattered landscape through an eighteen-inch hole in the shielding a little above my left shoulder. But I was able to keep moving, despite a clanking noise and a heavy sway to the left, and I made it to the next sanctuary, a row of explosions trailing like knots in a kite tail behind me.

I had made it around halfway up the valley, which was about as good as could be expected. Maybe even better, all things considered. I nosed in close again, bore to the right. I pulled out at the far end, where I was screened by an overlapping mass of boulders about fifty feet ahead. I made my way up to them and kept bearing right, until I had gone about as far as I could go without exposing myself. This was about two hundred yards beyond my previous shelter, which was then taking quite a pounding. I had no idea what the layout was on the other side, so I decided to investigate on foot.

I left everything running, including the radio, with its faint, importuning, "Are you there, Angel? Are you still there?" and I climbed down onto the rocky ground, feeling its continuing vibrations through my armor, and I smelled burning chemicals and tasted salty dust.

I circled carefully, keeping close to the boulder, dropping to my belly and crawling the final distance as I rounded it. As I did this, I picked up Styler's voice on my suit-radio.

"I'm sorry it had to be this way, Angie," he said. "If you are still alive and can hear me, I hope you believe that. For whatever it is worth, everything that I said was true. I was not lying to you . . ."

Yes! If I brought it around to the right and up that

sharp upswing, I would have a clear line of fire! If I got all the rockets off, there was a sharp downgrade I might be able to reach. It led to what looked like a dried-out streambed . . .

". . . I am just going to keep firing now until nothing remains. You have left me no alternative . . ."

I made my way back to the vehicle and rechecked all systems. The rocks behind me would soon be a gravel pit. Or sand.

Everything was ready. Any second now he might throw something really heavy this way, too. I had to be fast.

I clanked forward and up at a respectable speed. At times, the list almost made it seem as if I were about to topple to the left.

I made it, though, had a momentary, clear view of the Doxford headquarters, flameless now, but emitting a great plume of gray smoke, and then I halted, locked in and fired my rockets, one after the other, each jolt threatening to knock me back down the slope.

I did not wait to see the result, but plunged ahead the moment the last missile had been discharged.

I reached the bottom of the downgrade, swung left and kept going. Very soon thereafter, the rise from which I had fired erupted in flame and was reduced to a smoldering crater. A shower of gravel pelted me moments later.

I continued undisturbed for what seemed a long while. The firing continued, but it fell in a random pattern now and seemed a trifle more sporadic than it had been.

I could not leave the gulley at the rock-shrouded spot I desired. I tried, but the engine was not able to haul me up the slope. Its clanking had grown more ominous, also; and I detected the smell of burning insulation.

When I finally reached the only grade it could take, I pressed on up it and discovered that I was within four hundred yards of Styler's citadel.

The near side of the building had caved in completely, and I could see flames dancing beyond the rubble. There was more smoke than before. The guns—wherever they were, whatever sort they were—went crazy briefly, then fell silent. This lasted for perhaps ten seconds. Then one of them commenced firing again, slowly, regularly, at some imaginary target far off to the right and back. A long line of squat, heavy-treaded robots was drawn up before the building, absolutely still, presumably guarding the place.

"All right, you were lucky," Styler said, and his voice sounded strange after the long silence. "I cannot deny the damage you have done, but you have come about as far as you can. Believe me, it is a lunatic mission. Your vehicle is about ready to break down and the robots will swamp you. Your death will be useless to anyone, damn it!"

The robots began to roll toward me then, raising what were obviously weapons. I opened fire on them.

The sound of his breathing filled the cabin as I advanced, shooting, and the robots did the same.

I destroyed about half of them before the vehicle collapsed and began coming apart around me. One of the guns still worked, though, so I stayed with it, firing, adjusting the devices on my armor the while. I was hit quite a few times personally, but the suit held fairly well against the laser slashes and the projectiles.

"Is there really someone there?" Styler finally said. "Or have I been talking to a machine? I thought I heard you laugh earlier. But hell! That could have been a recording! Are you really there, Angel? Or is something that knows nothing of it in the process of crushing a reed? Say something, will you? Anything. Give me some sign there is an intelligence out there!"

The robots had divided themselves into two groups and flowed toward me in a sort of pincer movement. I hammered away at those on the right until my gun was destroyed. I damaged four of them before this happened, and the grenade that I threw as I leaped from my burning wreck took out three more.

I ducked behind the hulk, hurled a grenade at those to the left, slapped together my laser gun, moved to the right again, began firing at the nearest machine.

It took too long to burn it to a stop, so I slung the gun, threw another grenade, came out running. I might be able to run fast enough to hold a lead on an uphill course. I was not certain.

Three of the dozen or so remaining robots could not be avoided, so I had to stop and grapple with the nearest. It had snagged me with a long cablelike appendage as I tried to get by it.

33

Hoping that the prosthetic strength augmentation would be sufficient, I caught hold of it low and struggled to raise it above my head. I managed this just as the next tried to close with me, so I brought the one down upon the other as hard as I could, stopping them both, pushed the third over onto its side and ran.

I made thirty or forty yards before their fire knocked me over and their beams made the armor more than just uncomfortably warm.

"At least you appear to be human," came Styler's words, on my suit radio. "It would be terrible if there were nothing inside, though, like one of those evil, hollow creatures in Scandinavian legends—an empty presence. God! Maybe you are! Some piece of a nightmare that didn't go away when I woke up . . ."

By then I had a grenade ready, and I threw it back at my pursuers and followed it with my second-to-last one. Then I was on my feet and running toward the heaped rubble that lay before the building. It was about thirty yards and I felt their beams upon me and I was knocked down and got up and staggered on, feeling the burning at all points where my armor contacted my body, smelling my sweat and cooking flesh.

I dove behind a pile of masonry and began tearing at the clasps to my armor. It seemed to take me ages to get out of it, and I bit partway through my lip while holding back a scream. The headpiece addressed me in Styler's voice as it fell to the ground:

"Do you not think the human race is worth saving? Or worth the effort, the attempt, to save it? Do you not feel it deserves the opportunity to exercise its potentials in the full—"

It was smothered then beneath a slide of rubble as I clawed my way forward into a firing position, not bothering to check my burns, bringing the laser to bear on the nearest of the advancing robots. There were three of them still in action, and I held the beam upon the foremost for an intolerably long while before I burned a hole through its turret and it came to a sputtering, smoking halt.

I shifted it to the second one immediately, and it occurred to me then that they had not necessarily been designed for combat purposes. They were not sufficiently specialized. It seemed as if he had marshaled and armed a horde of multi-use machines and sent them against me. They could have been designed to move faster and perform with deadlier efficiency. Their weapons were not really built into them, but borne by them.

"Of course the race is worth saving," I said through the taste of salt. "But whenever circumstances conspire against it, its own irrationality pushes it forward for the kiss. This madness is its doom. If it were mine to do, I would beat it out, breed it out." I laughed then, as the second robot came apart. "Hell! I'd start with myself!"

I could hear the crackling of flames at my back, as well as the swishing of a sprinkler system. I had my beam on the final robot now, and I was beginning to fear I had gotten to it too late. Its own beam was melting and pulverizing my heap of protective junk, and I kept ducking my head and pulling it to the side, blinking dust from my eyes, blowing it from my nose, smelling my burning hair and my charred ear.

It came, it came, it came. My left hand seemed to be on fire, but I knew that I would not move until one of us was extinguished by the blaze.

I kept firing after it had stopped, I guess, because I had my eyes squeezed shut by then and my head turned to the side, and I did not see it happen.

When I realized that too much time had passed for me to be alive if things had not gone right, I stopped firing and raised my head. Then I let it fall again and just lay there, knowing it was all right now, aching, unable to move.

After perhaps half a minute, I knew that I had to get up and go on, or I would just lie there losing the benefit of all that adrenalin, growing weaker and sleepier before my pain and fatigue. I pushed myself upright, reeled back. I almost fell as I stooped to retrieve my final grenade from its place at the hip of my armor. Then I turned and faced the building.

The large metal doors were closed. When I moved to them and tried them, I found that they had been secured. While I had knocked many holes in the building, fires seemed to be burning behind all of them. I backed away, half-expecting an explosion when I tried it, raised my gun and burned away the locking mechanism.

Nothing happened. No hidden charges.

I moved forward, opened one of the doors, entered.

It was a simple lobby, of the sort to be found in office buildings anywhere. Deserted, though. And hot and smoky.

I stalked ahead, ready to fire at the first movement of anything, wondering about concealed guns, bombs, gas nozzles, hoping they were damaged now or powerless, if present, and going over the plans for the place which I held in my mind.

My feelings were that he would be downstairs in the brain room. It was the safest as well as the most sensitive place in the entire installation.

As I worked my way toward the rear of the building in search of a stairwell, Styler's voice came to me over the loudspeaker system:

"I was not mistaken about you," he said. "I was afraid of you from the first. It is a pity that we could only meet under these circumstances. You possess a quality I admire greatly—your determination. I have never seen such a singlemindedness, such a definition of purpose before. Once you made up your mind to take the contract on me, that was it. You closed it to everything else at that moment, and nothing short of death will stop you now ..."

I dashed through a burning corridor, leaped over a section of fallen wall. Sprinklers soaked me as I went.

"... We were miscast, you and I, you know? Have you ever considered what would have happened had Othello been faced with Hamlet's problem? He would have dealt with matters as soon as he had spoken with the ghost. There would only have been the one act and no great tragedy. Conversely, the Dane could have resolved the poor Moor's dilemma in a twinkling. It is sad that such things continue to be so. Had I been in your place, I would be in control of COSA by now. They were in terrible shape. Seriously. This assault on Doxford is part of their death throes. Their top management hated one another more than they did their competitors. You could have exploited your ruthless grandfather-image and moved right in, then bullied them into line. You— Oh, hell! It doesn't matter now, I have answers for everybody's problems but my own. If you sat where I sit, knew what I know, you might have been able to stop the war. I didn't, though, so why talk about it? I was still busy weighing

36

alternatives when the bombs were going off. You would have done *something* . . ."

The door to the stairwell was jammed shut. I burned it and kicked my way through. Smoke billowed out, but I held my breath and plunged ahead.

". . . And I am still thinking, considering the possible ways of handling the present situation . . ."

I groped my way about the first landing, continued on down, my eyes stinging and watering.

The door at the foot of the stair was locked. I burnt away the lock plate, my head spinning, blood hammering in my temples. Another flaming corridor confronted me. I ran its length, blasted another door and entered a hot but unfired hallway.

I hurried, cutting my way through several more doorways, expecting an explosion, a round of gunfire, the hiss of gas at any moment. The air grew cooler, cleaner, as I proceeded, finally approaching something I considered normal and comfortable. The lights burned steadily, and though there were communication boxes at regular intervals, the only sounds that emerged were those of heavy breathing and whispers, possibly curses, that I could not quite make out. I wondered—had wondered all along—whether he was alone. I had not yet encountered a single human being, living or dead, on Alvo, and while it seemed likely that any others would have headed for his sheltered area when the attack began, the monologue-like quality of Styler's speech would tend to indicate that he was alone and possibly had been so for some time. Where, then, was everybody else? This was a big place, with a supposedly large staff.

Soon, though, the matter would be resolved. I caught sight of the heavy door that marked the entrance to his sanctuary.

I approached cautiously, found it to be sealed, as I had expected. I raised my gun and began to burn it.

The charge gave out before I had finished, though. The lock still held too well.

I had the grenade, of course. But if I were to use it to blow the door, I would be disposing of my only weapon capable of killing at a distance. The only thing I would have left beside my hands would be a stiletto I had picked up in Sicily. My instructors had laughed when I had

37

insisted on bringing it along. They did not believe in good-luck charms.

I drew it from my boot, casting the gun aside. I located the grenade.

"I imagine you expect to be picked up by your associates after you have completed your mission," Styler said, his voice coming from a speaker above the door. "When they fail to come for you, you may begin to wonder whether you have been abandoned or whether perhaps I spoke the truth concerning the war on Earth. I spoke the truth. Then you will look for some means of departing Alvo on your own. You will find that there seems to be none available. You will begin to suspect that you are the only human being on the planet. This will be correct. Then you will wish that you had believed me, for you will realize that with me you slew the solutions to your various dilemmas."

I backed down the hall, threw the grenade and ducked into a recessed doorway.

"I have sent everyone else away. You see, I saw this coming months ago. Now, with the war, it is doubtful that any will be returning. The refugees are being sent to those worlds where settlement had already be—"

The explosion, in that confined area, sounded enormous. I was out of my niche and running before the echoes had died, the vibrations ceased, before all of the rubble had hit the floor.

If he had indeed sent everyone else offworld, it indicated that there was no one to come pick me up, had I halted at any point in my expedition as he had requested. Therefore, he had simply wanted a stationary target. The hell with him! Any possible beginnings of sympathy quickly vanished.

I plunged across the blasted threshold, my stiletto low and ready.

I did not stop moving once I had entered, but took in my surroundings as I made my dash. No splash of Renaissance splendor, as I had half-anticipated. The far wall was the face of an enormous console, the near one housed a multitude of screens, showing various views of the valley and the building's burning interior. The front of the room was separated from the rear by a decorative screen, was carpeted and furnished for full-time residence.

Styler, looking as he had in the pictures, was seated at a small metal desk, near to the left wall. An elaborate machine, possibly some extension of the behemoth at the rear of the room, jutted from the wall to enclose him on the right. His head was bared, and a mass of leads ran from it to the unit. He was staring at me, and he held a gun in his right hand.

I did not know how many times I was hit until afterward. I believe the first shot missed me. I am not certain about the second one. It was a small-caliber weapon and he managed to fire it three times before I knocked it aside, plunged my blade into his midsection and watched him sag back into the seat from which he had risen.

"You will—" he began, then opened and closed his mouth several times, a look of surprise breaking, for an instant, the grimace he had worn.

His right hand shot out, threw a small switch on the panel at his side. He slumped forward then, across the desk top, twitching.

On the corner of his desk, near to where I was leaning, breathing heavily, there was a telephone. It began ringing.

I stared at the thing, fascinated, unable to move. It was ridiculous, absurd, that it should be ringing. I fought back a wild impulse to laugh, knowing that it would do me no good, that it might take me a long while to stop.

I had to know. I would always wonder, if I did not find out now.

I reached out and raised the receiver.

"—discover possible solace," his voice continued, coming now through the earpiece, "in the building at the other end of this valley."

I controlled a sudden desire to scream, I maintained my grip on the receiver. With my other hand, I reached out and grasped his shoulder. I pushed him back in the chair. He was either dead or so close to it that it made little difference.

"The neurons are still firing," came his voice through the phone, "and with my hookup, I can activate anything here that still functions, even though my own vocal cords are now beyond my control. Everything here goes through the formulator, and its voice is my own.

"You will have to study what you find in the other

39

building. It will not be easy. You may well fail. The alternative is to spend the rest of your days alone in this place. But there are teaching devices, records, my notes, books. You have nothing but time now, in which you may make the attempt or not, as you choose. So far, I have anticipated everything correctly. I feel that this is about as far as I can go—"

There came a click, followed by a dial tone.

I collapsed.

Here, here, there and again. The years, the clones, the gates ... I learned.

I studied the materials in what was to become Wing Null. I learned. The alternative was some worse form of madness than the one I already knew. I had to get out of there, try to find Julia, do something.

Jigsaw and evening star ...

I got out of there. I never located her grave, if she had one, but I was able to establish that she was not one of those who had made it into the House, whose Wings existed on the outworlds which were not quite ready for man.

I got out of there. There was a lot of forgetting that I wanted to do, and having had an abundance of time for introspection I could even be specific about it. I possessed the techniques for pinpointing everything I disliked about myself and erasing it from my mind. I decided to do it. I wished it might be done for the whole human race—what was left of it—and decided there might be a way to do that, too. Only it would take more time, a process of moral evolution, with me there to guide it and evolve along with the others, staying only one step behind, as I saw it, to take care of the dirty work, for which I was well suited. This pleased me. I destroyed a portion of myself and soldered pin one in its place. Later ones might be pulled in an emergency, but I wanted Angelo di Negri to stay dead. I hated him. Then I activated the clones, and we could trust us completely.

We got out.

Part II

1

As I felt the bullet enter my heart, my first reaction was an enormous bewilderment. How—?

Then I was dead.

I do not remember screaming, though Missy Vole said I did, and clawing wildly with my right hand. Then I stiffened, relaxed, was still. She was in the best position to know, poor girl, as it happened in her bed.

A crazy thought ran through my mind just before I died: *Pull pin seven* . . . Why, I had no idea.

I remember her face, green eyes mostly hidden behind long lashes, pink lips slightly parted in a smile. Then I felt the pain and the bewilderment, not hearing but seeming to have just heard the shot that killed me.

A doctor was later to tell me that I had sustained no cardiac damage, despite the symptoms I had exhibited, that there was no apparent reason for my experiencing chest pains and blacking out. I was already aware by then that this was the case, and I just wanted to get away from the Dispensary and go direct to Wing 18 of the Library, cubicle 17641, to deal with the aftermath of my passing.

But they detained me for several hours, insisting that I rest. The fools! If there was nothing wrong with me, why should I rest?

And I was unable to rest, of course. How could I? I had just been murdered.

I was quite frightened and very puzzled. How could anyone do such a thing? And, as an afterthought, why should they?

As I lay there, surrounded by antiseptic whiteness, alternately perspiring and shivering, I knew that I had to go, I wanted to go, to see what had been done to me, to cover it over quickly. But I also experienced a tremendous revulsion and physical fear of the sight, the evidence of

43

the act. This occupied me for a long while, and I made no effort to depart. I was sufficiently rational to realize that I would be useless until these initial feelings had eased.

So I rode with them, forced myself to think about them. Murder. It was virtually unheard of these days. I could not recall when last a murder had been committed, anywhere, and I was in a better position than most to be aware of such matters. Early conditioning and plenty of violence-aggression surrogation had a lot to do with it, as well as considerable medical expertise when it came to patching up the victim of a pathological outburst. But a cool, premeditated killing, such as mine had been . . . No, it had been an awfully long while. Some more cynical ghost of an earlier self whispered in my ear that it just might be that the real cool, premeditated ones were so well done that they did not even look like murder. I quickly banished him to the oblivion he had earned long ago. Or so I thought. With the quality of information maintained on everyone in the House, it was next to impossible.

It was especially unfortunate that it had to be me. I was now required to do what I had just dismissed as inconceivable in another. That is, find a way of concealing the fact that it had occurred. But after all, I was a special case. I did not really count—

The chuckle unnerved me, coming as it did from my own throat.

"Well said, old mole!" I decided within me. "I suppose there is a certain element of irony involved."

Crap! You have no sense of humor at all, Lange!

"I appreciate the incongruity of my position. But I do not consider murder a laughing matter."

Not when we are the victim, eh?

"You employ the wrong pronoun."

No, but have it your way. You are as red-handed as any.

"I am not a killer! I have never murdered anyone!"

I suppressed the beginnings of another chuckle.

What about suicide? What about me?

"A man has the right to do as he would with himself! You? You are nothing! You do not even exist!"

Then why are you so disturbed? Psychotic, perhaps? No, Lange. I am real. You killed me. You murdered me.

44

But I am real. And there will come a time when I will be resurrected. By your own hand.

"Never!"

It will be because you will need me. Soon!

Choking with fury, I rebanished my sire to his well-deserved limbo.

For several moments I cursed the fact that I was what I was, realizing simultaneously that this, too, was a pathological outburst brought about by the death-trauma. Before very long, it passed. I knew that so long as people remained people, it was necessary that I endure, in whatever form the day required.

We should be waiting for me to move. I knew that, too. Waiting and covering. The longer it took me to act, the more difficult things could become in the normal course of human surveillance. We all knew that, but we appreciated the scope of my feelings and understood that there would have to be a delay before I could function coherently again.

I ground my teeth and clenched my hands. This self-indulgence could be costly. It would simply have to be postponed.

I forced myself to get up and cross the room, to regard the gray-haired, dark-eyed reflection of my fifty-some years in the mirror that hung above the basin. I ran my hands through my hair. I smiled my lopsided smile, but it did not look too convincing.

"You are a hell of a mess," I told myself, and we nodded agreement.

I ran the water cold, sluicing the cracked pavements of my face, washed my hands, felt slightly improved. Then, trying hard not to think of anything but the immediate task, I fetched my clothes from the wall-slot and dressed. Once I had begun moving, there arose a compulsive need to continue. I had to get out of there. I rang for attention and began pacing. I paused several times at the window and looked out at the small, enclosed park, empty now of all but a few patients and visitors. High overhead, the lights had already entered the dimming cycle. I could see three corkscrewing jackpoles and the wide balconies of an arcaded area far to my left, the glint of enclosure-facings in the shadows to their rear. Traffic on the belts and

45

crossovers was light, and there were no special airborne vehicles in sight.

A sudden nurse fetched me the young doctor who had said earlier that there was nothing wrong with me. Since we were now in apparent agreement on this point, he told me that I could go home. I thanked him and departed, discovering that I actually felt better as I walked down the ramp and headed for the nearest beltway.

At first, I did not really care which way I moved. I simply wanted to get away from the Dispensary, with all its smells and reminders of that unfortunate state through which I had so recently journeyed. I slid by enormous medical supply depots, airborne ambulances occasionally passing overhead. Walls, dividers, shelves, pilings, platforms, ramps—all were white and carbolic about me. I edged my way inward and onto the fastest belt. Orderlies, nurses, doctors, patients and relatives of the deceased or ailing slipped by me with increasing speed and good riddance. I hated the place with its caches of medical stores, clinical subdivisions and supervised residences for the recovering and those headed in the other direction. The belt flowed through the corner of a park where such unfortunates waited, on benches and in power chairs, for the day when the black door would open for them. Overhead, birdlike power cranes transported units of people and machinery, to maintain the perpetually recomputed requirements of the shifting people:things:power: space equation, moving with but the faintest clucking amid the great crosshatchery in the sky. I changed belts a dozen or so times, not drawing another easy breath until I was well into the crowded, daylighted Kitchen, with its smells and movements and sounds and colors to remind me that I was a permanent part of this and not that other.

I ate in a small, brightly lit cafeteria. I was very hungry, but after the first minute or so the food became tasteless and its chewing and swallowing mechanical. I kept glancing at the other diners. Unbidden, the thought came into my mind: Could it be one of them? What does a murderer look like?

Anybody. It could be anybody ... anybody with a motive and a capacity for violence, neither of which appears on a person's face. My inability to think of anyone

46

possessing these qualities did not alter the fact that they had been exercised a few hours earlier.

My appetite vanished.

Anybody.

It was a hell of a time to go paranoid, but I felt the sudden need to move again, to get away. Everything about me had assumed a sinister aspect. The casual gestures and glances of the other diners grew menacing. I felt my muscles tense as a fat man with a tray passed behind me. I knew that if he bumped my chair or brushed against me I would leap to my feet, screaming.

As soon as the aisle was clear I got up. It was all I could do to keep from running as I headed back to the beltway. Then I simply rode for a time, mindlessly, not wanting to be in a crowd, but not wanting to be alone either. I heard myself cursing softly.

There was of course a place where there would be people, where I could be unafraid. I felt fairly certain of that. There was an easy way to find out, but my mood might be communicable and I wanted to keep it to myself until it went away. The easiest thing to do was simply to go there—to the scene of the murder.

I decided that I wanted a drink first. But I was not about to order one in this Wing. Why? Again the irrational. I had been discomfitted in my own chambers.

I followed the overheads, belting to the nearest subway station.

Finally, I saw in the distance the towering wall with its changing pattern of lighted numbers and letters. I disembarked at the station and studied the departures. A small number of people trickled through the incoming gates and others stood about or sat in the bleachers, keeping an eye on the board. Studying the thing, I learned that Gate 11 would take me to the Cocktail Lounge of Wing 19 in six minutes. I entered the cage at 11—there was no line—and presented my card for scanning. There came a humming followed by a click, after which the meshed door in the rear opened.

I passed through and headed up the ramp to the waiting area by the Gate. There were three men and a girl there. The girl had on a nurse's uniform. One of the men—an old codger in a power chair—might have been in her care, though she was standing quite a distance from him. He gave me a brief, sharp look and a faint smile, as though he might be interested in striking up a conversation. I glanced away, still feeling antisocial, and moved to a position far to his left and forward. Of the other two men, one stood near the Gate, his face partly hidden by the paper he was reading, and the other paced, briefcase in hand, his eyes on the clock.

When the red active light came on, accompanied by a buzzing sound, I waited for the others to pass through before I moved toward the Gate.

I submitted my card for rescanning and moved through the entranceway. As I entered the subway, I could hear a faint crackling all about me and the smell of ozone came into my nostrils. A hundred or so yards of metal-lined tunnel lay ahead of me, faintly illuminated by dirty overhead glow-plates. A haphazard array of advertisements and graffiti covered the walls, random bits of litter dotted the floor.

Halfway along the tunnel, a short, swart man stood reading a poster, hands clasped behind his back, mouth working around a toothpick. He turned and grinned at me as I approached.

I edged my way over to the left, but he headed toward me then, still grinning. As he drew near, I halted and folded my arms across my chest, the fingertips of my right hand separating the mag-bound seam of my jacket beneath my left armpit and coming into contact with the tiny butt of the tranquilizer pistol I carried there.

His grin became more conspiratorial, and he nodded it, saying, "Pictures."

Before I could respond, he had drawn open his jacket and was reaching inside. I relaxed, for I saw that he was not going for a weapon, but did indeed have a sheaf of photos sticking up out of an inside pocket. He withdrew them and took a step nearer, shuffling them slowly.

Anywhere else, some other time, and I might have arrested him or told him to get lost, depending on my mood. But there, in the territory-less way through subspace, the question of jurisdiction was always tricky. It would be especially complicated if he had been waiting around through several shiftings, as I suspected he had. Also, I was off duty and all out of professional feelings at the moment. I moved to the right, to go around him.

He clutched at my arm and thrust his pictures before me.

"How about that?" he asked.

I glanced down. My mood must have been even more pathological than I had estimated, for I kept looking as he played slowly through his glossies.

For reasons I did not attempt to analyze, I found myself fascinated by the display, though I had seen all of them in some variation or other countless times in the past.

There were three deep-space shots of the Earth, one each of the other planets, perhaps a dozen of planets in other solar systems and a score of star groups. I was strangely moved by them, and slightly irritated with myself for feeling that way.

"Nice, huh?" he said.

I nodded.

"Fifty," he said. "You can have the whole lot for fifty dollars."

"Are you crazy?" I said. "That's too much."

"They are very good pictures."

"Yes, they are," I said. "But they are not worth that much to me. Besides, I don't have fifty."

"You can have any six for twenty-five."

"No."

I could simply have said I never carried cash and ended things right there. Theoretically, there was no need for cash, since my i.d. card was also good for charging anything against my personal account, the balance of which was instantly verifiable. But everyone, of course, carries some cash, for purchases he does not wish recorded. I could also have told him to go to hell and kept walking.

All right, I was stalling for some reason. The reason must be that I was attracted by the photos. In the interest of dealing with my post-death trauma as expeditiously as possible, I decided to humor my neuroses and buy a couple.

I selected a crisp, clean shot of the Earth and one of the black and bright sprawl of the Milky Way. I gave him two dollars apiece for them, tucked them away near my pistol and left him there with his toothpick and his grin.

49

A few moments later I stepped into the Cocktail Lounge in Wing 19.

I moved down the ramp and out of the station. I mounted the beltway. It was always evening here, and I found it comfortable for that reason. The ceiling was invisible in the darkness, and the little areas of light were like campfires in a vast field. I remained on the slow belt and had it pretty much to myself. The four who had preceded me through the Gate were nowhere in sight. I transferred several times, making my way toward one of the darker areas, far in toward the left. I passed among the carefully contrived nooks and adyts, done up in all manner of motifs, some of them occupied, many of them not. Here and there, I came upon a party and could sometimes hear the strains of music and the sounds of laughter. Occasionally, I glimpsed a couple, fingertips touching, heads close together above a small table on which a tiny light flickered. Once I caught sight of a solitary figure, leaning heavily on his table, drinking in the dark. I must have proceeded for several miles before a satisfactory sense of seclusion enfolded me and I stepped down to seek my own place.

I made my way among darkened tables, turned a corner, crossed over a small bridge and passed through a cluster of fake palm trees, moving quickly to escape the Polynesian decor. Several more turnings, and I came to a surprising little place. Settling myself onto a chair with a cross-stitch seat at the side of a small table, I leaned forward and turned on the imitation oil lamp. Its soft, yellow light showed me armchairs with lace antimacassars on their backs, an upright piano, a pair of expressionless portraits, a shelf of expensively bound books. I had wandered into a Victorian drawing room, and it struck me as just the mood-easer I needed, eminently solid and secure.

I sought the ordering unit, located it beneath the table. Inserting my card, I ordered a gin and tonic. As an afterthought, I requested a cigar. A moment later, they arrived and I lifted the hatch and brought them to the tabletop.

I took my first cool sip and lit the cigar. Both of them tasted fine. I stopped thinking for a short while and simply sat there wrapped in a pleasant feeling. Something finally stirred down at the bottom of my mind, though, and I slipped my hand into my jacket and withdrew the two photos. I placed them side by side on the tabletop and regarded them.

Again, the fascination and something strangely like nostalgia for these unseen things . . .

As I pondered the Earth and that great river of stars, I attempted to analyze these feelings. Failing this, an uneasiness came over me, rising to a near-certainty as to their origin.

Old Lange, my late senior . . . It had something to do with him, the sacrificed part . . .

But there was only one way to find out for certain—an emergency procedure which I could not recall ever having been used. Even though a terrible, frightening thing had happened to me, I did not see that an exploration of my post-traumatic reactions to some pictures warranted its employment. The dead were dead, and they were meant to remain so for very good reasons. While the present situation was quite serious, I could not conceive of any set of circumstances which would justify pulling pin seven—

My God! Like somebody I could not recall and his piece of spongecake, there came a sudden remembrance. My crazy, dying thought, smothered until that moment by the pain, the fear . . . *Pull pin seven* . . .

Why, I still had no idea.

There came no mocking chuckle, no delirious schizophrenic reaction. And I would have welcomed even that right then, for I felt completely alone with a fear so naked I could almost see the bones.

I was afraid of what it stood for, what it meant. Even more than death, I feared pin seven.

Why did I have to be the oldest, be the nexus? Why did the responsibility have to be mine?

I gulped my drink, not allowing myself to say, "It is not fair." There was a quick, easy way to relieve my aloneness, but this would not be fair to the others. No. I had to sweat and figure this part out for myself. It was the only way. I cursed my weakness and my fear, but knew there was no help for me this side of the black door. Damn it!

I ordered another drink, sipping this one slowly, and puffed on my cigar. I gazed at the pictures, trying to

51

penetrate their mystery by sheer eyeball power. Nothing. Attractive and *verboten*, nobody alive remembered what was left of the Earth, and who the hell had ever seen a star? Despite my age, I still felt somewhat guilty and self-conscious to be sitting there staring at a picture of the place we had come from and its galactic backdrop. However, my intentions were not prurient.

I thought that I heard a noise, but with all the partitions and furnishings it was impossible to determine its direction. Not that it really mattered, I suppose. There could be someone seated within a few feet of me, neither of us aware of the other's existence. Though I preferred the actuality, the illusion of solitude would be sufficient, I supposed. I was not yet ready to get up and move on.

I listened to the ticking of the clock in its glass case. I liked this little area. I would have to note down its coordinates so that I could come again. I—

I heard the noise, unmistakable this time, louder. Someone had bumped against a piece of furniture. But there was also a background sound now, an underlying accompaniment that was soft and whirring, mechanical. That was better. It meant that it was probably a robotic cleaner-upper, in which case it would avoid a functioning area.

I took another sip, smiling faintly as I moved my hand away from the photos. I had automatically covered them when I thought that someone might be coming this way.

After several moments, I heard it again, very clear, very near. Then he came into sight, rounding the corner at the far end of the room. It was the old man in the power chair who had preceded me through Gate 11. He nodded and smiled.

"Hello," he said, gliding forward. "My name is Black. I saw you at the subway station—Dispensary, Wing 3."

I nodded.

"I saw you, too."

He chuckled as he drew up beside the table.

"When I saw you get off the belt here I figured you were stopping for a drink." He glanced at my glass.

"I didn't see you on the belt."

"I was fairly far behind you. Anyway, I find myself in a slightly awkward position, and I thought you might be willing to help me."

"What is that?"

"I would like to buy a drink."

I gestured at the table.

"Go ahead. The unit is underneath."

He shook his head.

"You don't understand. I can't do it. Directly, that is."

"What do you mean?"

"Doctor's orders. My account is flagged. If I stick my card in that machine and ask for a drink, Central will order it not to sell me one when it runs the automatic credit check."

"I see."

"But I'm not broke. I mean, I have cash. Only, that thing has no use for cash. Now what I had in mind was this: If I could find someone who would buy me a drink on his card, I could reimburse him in cash—hell! I'd even buy him a drink, too!—and there would be no real record of my having done it."

"I don't know," I said. "If your doctor does not want you drinking, I'm not sure that I want to be responsible for something that might not be good for you."

He nodded.

"Oh, the doctor's right," he said. "I'm hardly the picture of health. Just look at me and you can tell that. It's no fun being in the shape I'm in. They keep me alive, but I'd hardly call it living. A little physical discomfort tomorrow is not too high a price for a stiff bourbon on the rocks. It won't kill me." He shrugged. "And even if it would, it would not matter to anyone. What do you say?"

I nodded.

"It's not illegal," I said, "and you are the only real judge of what is important to you."

I inserted my card in the slot.

"Make it a double," he said.

I did, and when I passed it to him he took a long, slow sip and sighed. Then he set the glass down, fumbled inside his jacket and withdrew a pack of cigarettes.

"I'm not supposed to have these either," he said, lighting one.

We sat in silence for perhaps a minute, sorting out our private feelings, I guess. Strangely, I did not resent the intrusion on the solitude I had gone so far to achieve. I felt sorry for the old man, doubtless alone in the world,

53

waiting around to die, finding pretexts to go off from whatever rest facility housed him and cadge an occasional drink, one of his few remaining pleasures. But it went beyond sympathy. There was animation, defiance, strength in his deeply lined face. His dark eyes were clear, his mottled hands steady. There was something comforting, almost familiar, about him. I was certain I had never met the man before, but our meeting here, this way, gave me an odd, irrational feeling that it had been somehow prearranged.

"What have you got there?" he asked, and I saw the direction of his gaze. "Feelthy pictures?"

My face grew warm.

"Well—sort of," I said, and he chuckled.

He reached halfway toward them, then met my eyes.

"May I?" he asked.

I nodded.

He picked them up, leaned back with them. His shaggy brows dropped toward a squint and he cocked his head to one side. He stared for a long while, his lips pursed. Then he smiled and placed them back on the table.

"Very good," he said. "Very good pictures." Then his voice changed. "See Earth and then die."

"I do not understand . . ."

"It is an old saying that I just made up. 'See Venice and die.' 'See Naples and die.' 'May you die in Ireland.' Many places once took such pride in themselves that they considered a visit there to be the greatest thing in anyone's life. At my age, one can be a bit more cosmopolitan. Thanks for letting me see the pictures." His voice hardened. "They brought back many memories. A few of them were even happy ones."

He took a large swallow of his drink and I stared at him, fascinated. He seemed to grow larger, he sat more erect.

It was not possible, though. It simply was not possible. But I had to ask him.

"Just how old are you, Mr. Black?"

Part of his mouth grinned as he snubbed out his cigarette.

"There are too many ways to answer your question," he said. "But I see what you are really asking. Yes, I have seen the Earth—actually, not just in pictures. I remember what things were like, before the House was built."

"No," I said. "That is physically impossible."

He shrugged, then sighed.

"Perhaps you are right, Lange," he said. He raised his glass and drained it. "It does not matter."

I finished my own drink, setting the glass down beside the photos.

"How is it that you know my name?" I asked him.

Reaching into his pocket, he said, "I owe you something."

But it was not money that he withdrew.

"See the Earth," he said, and, *"A rivederci."*

I felt the bullet enter my heart.

2

How—?

The music was swirling all about me, pumping, throbbing, and the lights were changing color faster and faster. Then it was time for me to come in on the clarinet. I managed it. Shakily, but sufficiently.

Before too long there was applause. Weak-kneed, I got through the bows. Then the bandstand darkened and I followed the others down.

As we moved around back, Martin's hand fell on my shoulder. He was the leader, stocky going to fat, three-quarters bald, heavy pouches under his pale, watery eyes. A very good trombone player and a nice guy, too.

"What happened to you up there, Engel?" he asked me.

"Stomach pains," I said. "Must have been something I ate. They were pretty bad for a couple minutes."

"How are you feeling now?"

"A lot better, thanks."

"Hope you're not getting an ulcer. They're no fun. Something been bothering you?"

"Yes. But it will be over soon."

"Well, that's good. Take it easy."

I nodded.

"See you tomorrow."

"Right."

I moved away quickly. Damn! I had to find a collapsing place in a hurry. Every second counted now. Damn! How could I have been so complacent, so blind? So stupid! Damn!

I slapped my instrument into its case, changed clothes in record time and ignored or avoided everyone and everything that might slow me as I made for the beltway. I got over into the fastest lane and began some evasive traveling. I switched belts at nearly every intersection. I

56

jackpoled down three levels and walked until I was fairly certain I was not being followed. Then I took to the belts again and worked my way toward the Living Room.

My sense of urgency was enormous by then, and I knew that I was near to the edge of hysteria. A small, hot core of anger was the only thing that kept my panic in check. Something I did not understand had reached me and struck me, twice. Then, almost without my realizing it, the anger was there, and I could feel it growing. It was strange and it was strong. I could not recall whether I had ever felt so before. I must have, since I recognized it and embraced it so readily. Whatever, it seemed to buoy me a bit. Perhaps it was this, that in its incipience had served to prevent my collapse this time around. I felt the slow beginnings of a desire to reach out and punish my murderers—for purposes of a personal accounting, rather than in the interest of justice. Though I recognized the aberrant nature of the impulse I did not seek to straitjacket it with self-discipline, for I had to have something to sustain me.

... And it was not an altogether unpleasant feeling.

Now the faintest of smiles quirked the corners of my mouth upwards. No, it was not a bad thing to be angry. It was a natural, human feeling. Everybody knew that. It almost seemed a shame to waste it on aggression surrogates ...

I stepped down into the Living Room and walked through section after section. People sat, stood, reclined, talking, reading, napping, listening to music, viewing tapes, and there was always a quiet nook for someone who wanted to be alone. I hurried across the soft carpeting, rounding corner after corner, passing through a great variety of periods and styles, hoping I would not encounter anyone who knew me.

Luck!

A small, deserted alcove, dimly lit ... a fat, green chair that looked as if it might recline ...

Sure enough. It did. I turned the light even lower and leaned far back. There were two entrances to the place and I could keep an eye on both, though I was certain I had not been followed.

The first thing I did was try to relax and decide who I was. It is gratifying that the nexus-mesh occurs so smoothly. You always wonder, I guess, what it will feel like. Then it happens and you still do not know. You only know that it worked.

I knew I was not the same Mark Engel I had been before the old man shot Lange. I was Lange, but Lange was also me. I mean, we were us. We had merged, more or less, with the shifting of the nexus, when his body was destroyed. It did not require a massive adjustment, since we had experienced the same phenomenon on a temporary basis countless times in the past. Now that it was for keeps, there were a number of things I had to do to tailor the arrangement, so to speak. But they would have to wait. We should have acted right away, after the first murder. Lange had dragged his heels, though, and it had proved fatal. I did not approve of his postponing an important action, regardless of his mental condition. I could feel this tendency warring with my own resolve even then. That part would be sacrificed—soon—when I inserted pin eight.

Although the identity situation would ordinarily have precedence, it would have to take second place this time around.

About three centimeters behind my eyes, that is where I seem to live. My mind, my consciousness . . . I tightened and relaxed, tightened and relaxed, there in my home. A mental heartbeat, a mindbeat . . . Then it was all diastole, and thoughts the mindblood flowing uncontrolled . . .

Then we were there and together—Davis, Gene, Serafis, Jenkins, Karab, Winkel and the others. Suddenly, I was all of us and we were all of us me. There was little hesitation as everyone slipped into place, recognizing the new position of the nexus. A good, comfortable, familiar feeling.

I saw through many eyes, heard many sounds, felt the weight of all of our flesh. It was as though we were one body, our various limbs in all of the Wings. All but two, that is. And in a very special sense we were but one body.

In a timeless moment, we were all of us aware of the conscious contents of all of our individual skulls. It was a brief eternity of realization, a plasmic state of being wherein our temporary surrender of individuality caused all of us to grow, instantly, by the sum of the new experiential units which had come to be since our most recent meshing, perhaps a month earlier.

There was fear, and my surprise at the fact that there was so little anger other than that which I had brought to the meshing. My anger was countered by an attitude of mild reproval, tempered by the awareness that I had just received the nexus and had not had time to make the necessary adjustments. Otherwise, the anger might have been washed away, submerged. As it was, I saw that they also feared any reaction that might affect me before my new personality had solidified. Good. I felt the same way about it.

The first death had been that of Hinkley, in the Library, Wing 18. We knew that it had occurred in cubicle 17641, his private living quarters there, as we had all become instantly aware of his terminal impressions. He was with us still, but he was unable to supply any clues as to the motives or identity of his slayer. We had all reacted differently to the death, in keeping with our private temperaments, but none of us had any notion as to the reason for the killing and no one had done anything about it yet. As for Lange's/my body, it still lay in the Victorian drawing room of the Cocktail Lounge of Wing 19, unless the old man had done something with it.

. . . And nobody recognized Mr. Black. No one knew him from anywhere. I assigned myself the task of running the search for him, as I would have access to the necessary equipment very soon.

Davis was in the Library, Wing 18, keeping an eye on cubicle 17641. He had already seen to it that the quarters were shown as vacant and the phone switched to automatic answering. It was decided that he should not enter yet, but continue his watch until Serafis could get there. Serafis was a medic and could file the necessary papers showing death from natural causes. Then the body would be taken to Winkel's funeral home and disposed of quickly.

Lange was a problem, though. It was not only that another natural-causes certification by Serafis would look peculiar, coming from a different Wing and so soon after Hinkley's—but Lange had just had a very thorough checkup and had been found to be in good condition.

It was decided that Winkel would go after the body and

59

dispose of the evidence while he was at it. He was in a position to make the pickup look legitimate if almost anyone else came upon the scene. The body would then be transported to Wing Null, causing it to vanish from known existence. There it would be frozen, until we decided upon its most suitable disposition. In the meantime, we would have Lange put on leave from his employment and use his card for transportation, meals and occasional small purchases, so that he would continue, officially, to exist.

All available evidence would of course be gathered for our own private investigation of the killings. The fear that we felt was very strong. It had to be more than coincidence that two of us had gotten it as we had, and we were unable to come up with any guesses as to the reason which were not absolutely chilling. The exercise was somewhat futile, so we agreed to break the mesh for the time being and get on with the necessary actions immediately. I was to proceed to Wing Null, to make the adjustments needed for a permanent arrangement between Lange and myself.

I blinked away the shadows of their thoughts and rose quickly. I brightened the light, paced off a few tentative steps, reevaluating myself now that I was me once more. Well, almost me.

As I saw it, someone was out to destroy the entire family. The motive was immaterial. The fact that the only two murders in recent times should be of family members was sufficient. There were not that many of us around. It indicated, to me, that what we had thought the best-kept secret in the House had somehow been found out—at least in part. Mr. Black was doubtless waiting, planning to strike again. I would begin seeking him from Wing Null as soon as I had taken care of my other business there.

And when I found him, what?

I pushed the question aside, still unwilling to consider the answer my anger was offering. Later, later . . .

And again the fear . . . Not only my distress at the thought that death might be waiting for me anywhere now—but the Lange/me fear of the partial suicide we were now constrained to commit. You are not supposed to look at it that way, any more than you consider the removal of a throbbing tooth to be a small death. But there it was, and we had to go do it now.

60

As I left the alcove, thinking along these lines, I do recall it passing through my mind that if we were capable of doing it to ourself ...

I did not retrace my way through the Living Room, but traveled a circuitous route in the other direction, coming at last to a slow, narrow side-belt which I rode for a time. A flat, towering partition lay to my left, covered with an abstract design, dark-toned and seemingly endless. To my right were great, semi-lit sections of the Living Room, resting people haphazardly distributed within.

When I switched to another belt, moving at right angles to the one I had ridden. I glanced back. There was a figure, several hundred yards to the rear, which had not been present when I had mounted the conveyance. I waited perhaps two minutes and looked again. He had switched also, was still there. In fact, he was nearer now, as he was walking on the belt.

I waited several moments and began walking myself. Most likely, he was quite innocent, but I considered no precaution unwarranted at that moment. I changed again at the next intersection, but refrained from looking back. I saw that we were headed toward a somewhat crowded area.

As we passed through that section of the Living Room, I stepped down beside a group of sofas, took a few paces and glanced back again.

Yes, he was on this belt now, and he was looking at me.

I turned, folded my arms across my breast and stared back at him. There were dozens of people about me, talking to one another, reading, munching snacks, playing cards. I felt quite secure in their presence. He must have thought I was, too, if he meant me harm, for he immediately looked away and continued on by. I felt a small satisfaction in watching him pass, a tribute to my alertness and ingenuity. This vanished as soon as I began to uncross my arms, when I realized that I had unconsciously parted the seam of my jacket beneath my left armpit and was fingering the nonmetallic tranquilizer gun we all carried there. Then the fear was there, full force, as I realized it had never, really, left me. Emotionally chastened, and stoking my anger in hope of sparking some courage to flame, I moved forward and remounted the belt.

I could still see the man, up ahead. I had gotten a fairly good look at him, what there was to see. He had shoulder-length brown hair and a slightly darker beard. He wore blue mirror-glasses, a matching jacket and white, knee-length trousers.

A flash of blue, as he glanced back . . .

I began walking toward him, my heart pumping heavily. It was suddenly very important to me—more important than my fear, even—that I obtain his reaction.

He turned away, stood still for perhaps half a minute, then looked back again. I had kept walking, continuing to close the distance between us. The second time he looked back, I raised my right hand and slipped it inside my jacket in the fiction-honored fashion of a man reaching after a deadly weapon.

He moved quickly then, stepping down from the belt and darting behind a partition that projected out near to its edge. It was only then that I noticed his limp. I had not detected it when he had been walking straight toward me, but he tended to favor his left leg.

I got off the belt immediately. It would not do to let it carry me right past him if he were armed himself. I hurried to my right, heading toward a different partition. So far as I was concerned at the moment, the fact that he had fled was sufficient to establish that he harbored nasty intentions toward me.

Slipping along the partition, I worked my way back and in, cutting through an empty alcove and moving behind another partition that formed one wall of a corridor that bore off to my left—his direction—and dead-ended into a three-walled section containing four sofas, miscellaneous chairs and tables and a crackling fireplace. I dashed across its width and ventured a quick look around the near corner.

There was no one in sight.

I could see into several deserted sections before my view was blocked by more partitioning perhaps a hundred and fifty feet ahead. There were five or six crannies and chambers into which I could not see, however.

Cautiously, I advanced, drawing my gun and palming it now. In the space of four or five minutes, I had worked my way through, discovering no one. A couple more minutes, and I was into the area where the man had fled, searching it carefully.

He did not seem to be about. He had had time to slip off in any of several directions. I felt quite uncomfortable as I stood there, considering it. He might be circling, slipping up behind me, lying in ambush. The thought occurred to me that there might even be more than one person involved, that perhaps I was supposed to see this fellow while another . . .

The safest thing for me to do, I decided, was to get out of there as quickly as possible, confuse any pursuit and beat it to Wing Null.

I worked my way back to the belt, waited until it bore a group of passengers abreast of me and climbed on, moving immediately to a position in their midst. I received some foul glances and fishy stares from passengers I pushed by and elbowed aside, but that was all I got as we slid on through the area. I was a near-impossible target where I stood.

". . . You are very rude," a husky, redheaded woman with blue eye makeup was saying.

I nodded my agreement and kept watching the furnishings and people we passed. The man was nowhere in sight.

About half a mile farther along, we came to an intersection and I switched over, heading off to the left. The people I had used for shields continued on, sending a few remarks after me. They had all been together, apparently—a party coming or going somewhere.

Traffic was heavier on the new belt, and before too long it bore me to a two-way, multilane beltway. Crowds of people, staler air and an increased sound level enfolded me. I got into its fastest lane and rode for several minutes. Then I began switching again, following signs to the nearest jackpole.

It was a down tube, transparent, echoing, forever screwing itself into the House. A small boy came rushing upward, laughing and looking back over his shoulder. I reached out and seized his arm. He attempted to pull away, then turned and glared at me. A moment later, a woman—presumably his mother—came puffing upward, red-faced and looking even meaner. She slapped him and took hold of his other arm.

"I told you!" she said. "I told you never to do that!"

Then she looked at me.

"Thank you," she said, "for stopping him. I don't know why they like to run up the down ones and down the up ones."

I smiled.

"Neither do I," I said, releasing my grip somewhat reluctantly.

They got off at the next level, Kitchen, and while she was saying, "Wait till I get you home!" the boy turned around and stuck his tongue out at me.

I tried to think what it must be like, to be a child, to have parents.

I continued on down to the next level, the Recreation Room, disembarked there and found a fast belt through the playing area. Every team sport I could think of seemed to be in progress somewhere in the field section. For a time, the beltway was elevated, and I could see for miles in all directions. Balls were hit, kicked, thrown, caught, dribbled, run with, on fields and courts, over nets, against walls, into cages. Banks of spectators cheered and stamped their feet; wide, towering boards flashed scores; overhead speakers emitted decisions and static. The ceiling was light blue, a pleasant, somehow appropriate color. At the moment, I could detect no crane activity upon that peaceful, gridded surface. Swimming pools glimmered, cast dancing ghosts on towers and stands. Air currents bearing smells of sweat and liniment swept by, seeking ventilation units into which they might retreat to cleanse themselves.

The belt was fairly crowded, so it was impossible for me to tell whether I was being followed. I began switching down to smaller and smaller beltlines, heading in the general direction of a dimmed area. Traffic fell off as I came upon long rows of tables featuring more sedentary pastimes. Small groups and solitary players sat at cards and board games. Some competed against themselves, some against machines, their luck, skill, knowledge taxed to whatever degree they desired. Dice fell, wheels spun, cards were shuffled and dealt, counters pushed about; pieces advanced, retreated, jumped, captured, were captured themselves; numbers were called out, bids were made, tricks taken; people bluffed, attacked, sought wins, points, stalemates, proceeded directly to Go without collecting two hundred dollars, some money often changing hands beneath the table. I am not much of a gamester myself.

The blue was beginning to darken overhead, the voices diminishing, when I heard a shrill, ringing sound: a phone in a callbox at the near end of a deserted aisle. A strange feeling, that: hearing it and seeing it there with nobody around to answer.

There was a jackpole deep in the dimmed area, glowing beads marking its crystal spiral. I transferred again, onto an empty, one-lane belt. There was a weak light every hundred yards or so, and maintenance machines bumped and hummed in the gloom on either side of me. I kept looking back over my shoulder to see whether anyone else had come onto the belt. No one had.

A moment or two later, and I came to another intersection, decided to switch again. The juncture-point was completely deserted. Motes of dust, disturbed by the cleaning machines, swirled in the yellowish light of the lamp on the corner tower. As I passed there, I heard the ringing once more. Another phone, in a recess at the tower's base, had commenced to jangle. I could hear its persistent summons for a long way down the line. It was sort of sad, the effort to reach someone who just wasn't there, or the trying in the wrong place—whichever it was.

I passed an empty polo field, the mechanical horses standing like a row of depressed statues. The dark surfaces of pools buckled constantly, like memories. Opened to the floor, gray sacks bulging and swaying above, mouths on rollers moved among lockers and gaming tables, consuming refuse. An ambulance rose from some distant bay or playing field and sped through the twilit air, red cross aglow. I slid by a couple embracing in an alcove. I would not even have noticed them if they had not moved suddenly when they became aware of me. They averted their faces. So did I. Then I passed a partition on which a painted "STARS" had not been completely obliterated. Checking behind me, I saw that I was still alone on the belt.

I switched again, bridged over a series of exposed conduits, got down and walked for two blocks to shortcut my way to a belt that headed straight for the jackpole. The area was very silent and virtually deserted. A few individuals advanced toward the pole from various directions, though none were emerging from it at the moment. Three men loafed about a candy and periodical stand nearby, and I had a feeling that I could replace Lange's photos there—or lay a bet, or make certain other unauthorized purchases.

A draft of warm air struck me as I entered the glowing tube and descended. I was probably all right now, had doubtless been quite safe since I had departed the Living Room. Nevertheless, considering its destination, I was determined to make a thorough job of my flight. To my knowledge, there had never been a question of pursuit when any of us had retreated to Wing Null before.

I emerged at the next level into a section of the Office that was just closing operations. The sight of all those people getting ready to call it a day reminded me just how tired I had grown. For a moment, I debated continuing down to another level to avoid the rush. But mingling with a crowd would help obscure my trail that much more, so I decided to go ahead.

I mounted the main beltway and a few minutes later a whistle blew and waves of humanity came toward me from every direction. I rode the middle lane, which was soon filled to capacity, and I was jostled, crushed, immobilized and borne helplessly along. I was squeezed into anonymity, however, which I kept telling myself made it all worthwhile.

Turning my head, I could see the seeming endless rows of desks from which these people fled, arrangements of phones, blotters, papers softening in the already dimming light. Soon the cleaner-uppers would begin their rounds among them. I speculated as to the work performed there each cycle, then quickly closed my mind. Better not to think about it.

I resolved to follow the path of least resistance, and the press of the crowd bore me from belt to belt for perhaps ten minutes before it eased, died down, left me to make choices on my own once more. Then I followed my previous inclinations and worked my way toward a hinterland.

Soon I was riding feeder-belts and moving near to a completely dimmed area of the Office. I tentatively set my objective as another down-jackpole, this one on the far side of the darkened space.

As I zigged and zagged my way in that direction, I became aware of a possible pursuer. I was not certain, but it seemed that one of the several figures far to my rear had changed belts with me several times. But my nervousness had subsided considerably, as though I only had a limited supply and had already used most of it. I changed again and waited. Eventually, one figure followed. According to my watch and my estimates as to beltspeed and the distance between us, he was in the proper position to be the same individual.

All right, that much resolved, I decided on a course of action: I would make a final attempt to lose him. If that failed, I would wait in ambush.

I headed into the darkness and he followed. Then I changed until I came to a short one and began running. I reached the next intersection and switched before he appeared. I ran again. This belt was longer, and I was feeling all of my forty-six years by the time I came to another intersection. But he was not behind me when I turned then either.

I stood still for a moment, breathing heavily. I could hear no unusual sounds. It was quite quiet, and sufficiently dark for my purposes.

I stepped down from the left side of the belt. Acres of desks lay before me, vanishing beyond the dark frontier of my vision as though extending into infinity. I moved toward them.

The jackpole was still a good distance away. I did not head directly for it, but moved off at a tangent, passing along an endless-seeming aisle through the work area. I ran by desk after shadowy, identical desk, until I was well back into the darkness.

Slowing to a walk when I was unable to run any longer, I found myself taken by an eerie treadmill illusion. The relentlessly recurrent sameness on either hand—small swivel chair, gray desk, green blotter, phone, in-basket, out-basket—all worked to create a sensation of nonmovement. There came a feeling of inescapability, accompanied by that odd intimation of eternity which sometimes occurs along with a monotonous stimulation of the senses, and for that timeless instant it seemed that I always had been and always would be running in place at the center of a universe of desks.

I stopped and leaned against one, to demonstrate its substantiality as well as to catch a moment's rest. Checking back toward the lighted belt trail, I saw no one. If anyone had been following me, I seemed to have given him the slip. There was no movement that I could detect among the dark hundreds of desks that I had passed.

Then, but inches away from my hand, the phone rang.

I screamed and began running. Everything that had been pent up, suppressed, pushed aside, ignored, forgotten, emerged in that awful instant.

I fled, a mindless bundle of perceptions and reactions; and pushing, hammering, driving even these apart, the ringing followed me.

. . . Pursued me, seemed to keep abreast of me—dying behind and breaking out afresh on each desk that I passed—my black-clad gorgons, wreathed by electric snakes. And this moment, too, seemed timeless and eternal.

I ran—wildly, madly—bumping into things, stumbling, cursing, no longer a man, but a frightened movement in a forest of menace. Some part of me seemed as if it might be aware of what was happening, but that did not benefit me in the least.

It—everything—was too much for me: the deaths, the menace, the pursuit, this assault by the unknown. I was afraid to look back. I might see something. Or, worse yet, see nothing. This was my breaking point, each ringing of the bells a fresh stab at the wound.

My breath came hard and hot into my chest, depositing a bit more of pain on each visit. My eyes and face felt moist; but then, I think my trousers were, too.

Through the wet kaleidoscope of my vision, far ahead, I seemed to see a light, a small, yellow halo—and perhaps that was a man bending within it.

Sobbing, I strove to reach it, whatever it might be— probably because it was warm and bright, so unlike everything else.

Then came the explosion that tore all sound from my ears, the flash of light that ripped the seeing from my eyes and the burning, body-rending shock that tore me to pieces, almost before the desperate words appeared on the screen of my mind: *Pull pin seven!*

Then everything ended.

3

Bone by weary bone, I came together again. I was uncertain as to where I was, what had happened or how long it had taken. I wanted to return to oblivion, rather than face whatever damage had occurred.

But consciousness was a persistent thing. It grew, rather than going away. I was just beginning to realize that I was still me and that I did not seem to hurt anywhere, when my eyes opened without any special planning on my part and began to focus.

"Are you all right?" said the voice from the fuzzy image less than a foot from my face, at once the most asinine and pleasant thing I had heard in a long while.

"I don't know," I said. "I just arrived. Give me a minute."

A great tidal wave of thought passed through my mind. I remembered everything that had happened, and I understood the last of it. Davis and Serafis were dead. Serafis had gone to Wing 18, as planned, and met there with Davis. Together, in the Library, they had entered cubicle 17641, Hinkley's residence. They tripped something that caused an explosion, killing them. I experienced their deaths.

I was surprised that I was still rational. I would not have believed that I could have remained so after going through the dying business four times in one day with extreme prejudice. Either I had grown emotionally numb, or I possessed greater resiliency than I had realized. Whichever it was, I was grateful that I was considerably less upset this time than I had been on the previous two occasions. Disturbed, naturally; concerned, of course. And very irritated.

I was lying on the floor, an arm about my head and shoulders, raising them. I was staring into a face that was near to my own, a girl's—and she looked more frightened than I felt, actually. I would not have called her pretty, although she had possibilities along that line—of the dark-haired, pale-eyed, high-cheekboned variety—but she was a doubly welcome sight when I considered the possible alternative. Her glasses were thick, colorless ovals and she wore no makeup. Whether it was concern or the glasses that so enlarged her eyes, I was uncertain.

"How are you feeling?" she said.

I nodded my head several times and struggled into a sitting position. I massaged my eyes, ran my hands through my hair and took a couple of deep breaths.

"All right now, thanks," I said. "It's all right."

She was kneeling beside me in the aisle. She had on black trousers and a gray shirt. She did not release her hold on my shoulders.

"What happened?" she said.

"I was just going to ask you that," I said. "What did you see?"

"You came running up the aisle. You screamed and fell."

"Did you see anyone else? Behind me? Near me? In the distance?"

"No." She shook her head slowly. "Was there someone with you?"

"No," I said, "I guess not. I thought I heard someone. It must have been you."

"Why were you running?"

"The telephones," I said. "It startled me when they all began ringing. Do you know why they acted that way?"

"No. They stopped about the same time I saw you fall. Some sort of electrical mixup, I guess."

I climbed to my feet, leaned against a desk.

"Would you care for a drink of water?"

I did not, but it would give me a chance to make up some lies, so, "Yes," I said, "that would be good."

"Sit down. I'll be right back."

She indicated the chair at the lighted desk. I went and sat in it while she hurried off somewhere to my left. I glanced down at the work spread out on the blotter. Pages of statistics and a pad full of longhand notes, which she seemed to be turning into some sort of report.

I searched in my pockets until I located a tiny pillbox

containing some capsules I sometimes used to keep me bright, alert and cheerful when playing a late stand. One could not hurt any and might do me some good, though I really wanted it as a prop.

When she returned with a cup of water, I said, "Thanks, I should have taken this earlier," and tossed off the capsule.

"How serious is it?" she said. "I can call—"

I shook my head and finished swallowing, satisfied that I had established my condition as fitting into some neat medical category.

"It is not as bad as it looked," I said. "I have these spells sometimes. I forgot to take my medication earlier. That's all."

"You're sure it's all over?"

"Yes. Everything is fine now. I guess I'll be moving along."

I started to rise.

"No," she said, placing her hands on my shoulders and pressing firmly downward. "You wait. Rest awhile."

"All right," I said, sinking back. "Tell me, why are you working here all alone?"

She glanced at the materials on the desk, blushed and looked away.

"I got behind," she said softly.

"Oh. Overtime, huh?"

"No, I'm doing it on my own."

"Sounds like real dedication."

Her lips tightened, her eyes narrowed.

"No," she said, "just the opposite." Then, "You don't work around here, do you?"

I shook my head.

"Well," she said, sighing, "I don't like what I do at all, and I am not very good at it. I got all confused, and I am way behind on everything. I came in on my own to see if I could get caught up."

"Oh. Sorry I interrupted you."

She shrugged.

"It's all right," she said. "I was just getting ready to quit when you came along."

"All finished?"

She smiled, faintly.

"You might put it that way."

71

"Oh?"

"Yes," she said. "In a few days they will find out, and my employment here will be terminated."

"I'm sorry."

She shrugged again.

"Don't be. I will go back to the unemployed labor pool, and maybe I will like the next job they find me better."

"How many have you had?"

"I forget. A couple dozen, I guess."

I studied her more closely. She only looked to be about twenty.

"Sounds pretty bad, doesn't it?" she said. "I'm not very good at anything. I'm accident-prone, too."

"Perhaps there is an error in your aptitude-profile," I said. "Maybe you should be doing a different sort of work altogether."

"Oh, they've tried me at damn near everything," she said. "They just sort of shake their heads now when they see me coming back." She chuckled. "What do you do?"

"I'm a musician."

"That is something I've never tried. Maybe I will sometime. What is your name?"

"Engel. Mark Engel. What's yours?"

"Glenda. Glenda Glynn. Mind if I ask you why you were walking through the Office in the dark?"

"Just felt like taking a walk," I said.

"You are in some sort of trouble."

I felt it strange that she had not at least put it as a question.

"What makes you say that?" I asked.

"I don't know," she said. "It is just a feeling that I have. Are you?"

"If I said yes, what would you do?"

"Try to help you if I could."

"Why?"

"I don't like to see people in trouble. I seem to be in it all the time myself and I don't like it. I'm a sympathetic person."

I could not tell whether she was joking or being serious, so I smiled.

"Sorry to disappoint you," I said, "but I am not in any trouble."

She frowned.

"Then you will be," she said. "Pretty soon, I'd say."

I was a trifle irritated by the amount of certainty she put into the pronouncement. Since I was just about to depart and doubtless never see her again, it should not have mattered. Somehow, though, it did.

"Just for curiosity's sake," I said, "would you mind telling me how you know this?"

"My mother told me it is because I am Welsh."

"That's crazy!"

"Uh-huh. But I'll bet you were thinking of going to the Basement when you leave here. You shouldn't, you know."

She must have read my bewilderment on my face, because she smiled. At least, I hoped she only read it on my face. I *had* been thinking of cutting through the Basement in my effort to rid myself of pursuit. She made me feel uncomfortable about it. She also cinched my decision to do it.

I snorted.

"That's silly. You couldn't know—"

"I told you."

"Well," I said, climbing to my feet, "thanks for your help. I am going to leave now." I could feel the pill starting to work, and it was the best I had felt in a long while. "I hope your next job is a better one."

She opened the desk's top drawer, swept all the papers into it and pushed it closed. I glimpsed an amazing entanglement of personal and business effects. Then she removed a sleeveless black jacket from the back of the chair, slipped it on and extinguished the desk light.

"I'm going with you," she said.

"I beg your pardon?"

"Maybe I can help," she said. "I feel sort of responsible for you now."

"That is ridiculous! You are not going anywhere with me!"

"Why not?"

I bit my lip. I could hardly admit that it might be dangerous when I had just been insisting on my trouble-free state.

"I appreciate your concern," I said, "but I'm all right now. I really am. There is no need for you to go out of your way—"

73

"No trouble," she said, taking my arm and turning me back toward the beltway.

It was only then that I realized she was just a little under six feet—just a few inches shorter than me—and very strong, despite a certain willowiness.

Suppressing several possible reactions, I considered the situation. It was possible that she had saved my life just by being where she was when she was. If it had been my pursuer's intent to panic me, he had succeeded admirably. Had he intended to administer the *coup* when I slipped over the edge of rationality, then Glenda's presence was probably what had stopped him. This being the possible case, I might be safer having her with me for a while. While I did not want to place her in jeopardy, I could not see, just off hand, any easy way to get rid of her yet. I would keep her with me for a few perambulations calculated to discourage pursuit, then leave her at the first opportunity and cut for Wing Null. Yes, that seemed best for all parties involved.

It troubled me that my adversary seemed to know me so well. It was not just that he was able to follow me so easily, but that he seemed to know precisely what sort of pressure to apply and when to apply it, to break me as readily as he had. I was beginning to wonder what it would take to stop him. Something extraordinary, I was afraid. Well, that could be arranged . . .

They seem to be getting closer.

"The sooner we get them in range, the better," I said within myself.

You are a better incarnation than Lange was.

"I know that."

But still not good enough, I fear.

"What do you mean?"

You are learning, but not fast enough. I think they will get you, too.

"Maybe. Maybe not."

It might not be a complete loss, though. You may learn something from the experience.

"Such as?"

Forget the dead and stop running. Get your enemy, then clean house.

"I have already established my own priorities."

A lot of good they are doing you.

74

"I will take your advice on forgetting the dead, though, beginning with you—"

Wait! You need me, you fool! If you want to live—

"Go!"

—pull pin seven ...

I completed the expulsion and sighed, "Some help I can do without."

"What did you say?" Glenda asked.

"Nothing," I said. "I was mumbling to myself."

"For a moment it seemed there was someone beside you."

"That is your Celtic imagination trying to justify its existence."

"No," she said, "that is what I pay it for."

I glanced at her then and she laughed. Peculiar sense of humor, that.

I was wary as we neared the beltway, but there was no one in sight this time either. We mounted it and were borne on through the gloom, side by side. Her presence seemed to have a stabilizing effect on me, a human anchor against my neurotic storms.

"How are you feeling now?"

"Better yet."

"Good."

After several minutes, we came to a crossway and switched to a larger belt. Our route was then better lighted and there were other travelers about. One more changeover and we would be headed toward the jackpole.

Pull pin seven ... It was an intriguing—if heretical—thought, to release whatever beasts Lange had enchained in the dark night of his soul. For a moment, I wanted to laugh, then felt offended, hurt and mildly amused in rapid succession. That part of me which had been plain old Engel found it very funny to think of prissy old Lange in such romantic terms. Because of his appearance, he often got the assignment of cruising about as an aging queen, picking up young men in need of rehabilitation. To think of him as wrestling nameless demons and then going through with a more than symbolic act of suicide in order to establish the nexus, was close to inconceivable to plain old Engel. That part of me which now was Lange had been hurt and offended. But already the divisions were beginning to blur, and I—whoever I was—reacted finally with only a mild amusement. It was good that the merger was proceeding so smoothly on the surface, though I wondered what conflicts might be raging in the greater, unconscious portion of my mind.

... To pull pin seven would be to undo Lange's greatest work in our continuing effort to direct the moral evolution of human consciousness. I did feel a certain tension as that which was Lange within me resisted my even thinking along these lines. That which was not, however, continued to speculate as to the nature of the sacrificed portion. It became a moth-and-candle thing. I had inherited Lange's personal demon, and he of course would like nothing better than to hear my shouted *Zazas, Zazas, Nasatanada, Zazas*, the words which fling wide the Gates of Hell ...

Where had I picked that up? Either from that portion of Hinkley which was mine, from Lange or from beyond pin seven, I decided. As if in answer, I could almost hear Hinkley's voice reciting something from Blake:

> But when they find the frowning Babe,
> Terror strikes thro' the region wide:
> They cry "The Babe! the Babe is Born!"
> And flee away on Every side.

I took it to be his answer to the diabolical metaphor for pulling pin seven. Since he had been the librarian, he had a good deal from which to choose. Upon reflection, though, did it represent approval or disapproval of the notion? There was no accompanying feeling to help me judge it. Ambiguity, I decided, was the trouble with literary types. I—

Damn! I pulled myself back from the distraction. Was the whole thing Lange's doing, an attempt to direct my thoughts away from my initial considerations?

Or was it he-who-had-been, attempting to whip up some enthusiasm for a resurrection?

What would I be like when my turn came?

I would play the clarinet to them, I decided—sweetly, yet with infinite pathos ...

I bit my lip. I stared out beyond the belt and marked our movement. I studied the curling of Glenda's hair behind her right ear and at the nape of her neck. I tapped my foot. It was time, I could tell, to shift my attention to externals. It had become too, too apparent that the conflicts within me were indeed stronger than they had seemed several jagged moments earlier.

"How far do you propose to accompany me?" I said.

"As far as is necessary."

"Necessary for what?"

"To see you safe," she said.

"That may be a bigger job than you think."

"What do you mean?"

"You were correct a while back when you said that I was in trouble."

"I know that."

"All right. What I am trying to say is that while you were right as to the condition, its degree is another matter. My trouble is serious and dangerous. You have already helped me more than you realize. Now that I am back on my feet and on my way again, I can best repay you by saying goodbye. There is really nothing more that you could do to help me along now, but if you were to remain with me the trouble could become contagious. So I thank you again, Glenda, and I will be leaving you at the jackpole."

"No," she said.

"What do you mean 'no'? I was not asking you. I was telling you. We have to separate. And very soon. You helped me. Now I am returning the favor."

"I have a feeling you will require additional assistance. Soon."

"It will be available."

"Yes. Because I will be there."

I rejected several possible retorts as we swept along, then, "Why?" I said. "Mind telling me why?"

"Because," she said, without hesitation, "I have never been involved in anything exciting before. All my life I have wanted to, but nothing ever happened. I was beginning to believe that nothing ever would. Then you appeared while I was sitting there knowing I was going to lose another stupid job. As soon as I heard the phones ringing and saw you running, I knew this was going to be something different. It almost seemed fated. The peculiar way the bells seemed to pursue you . . . your dramatic collapse—almost at my feet . . . It was very exciting. I have to know how it all turns out, you see."

"I'll call you when it's all over and let you know."

"I am afraid that will not be sufficient," she said.

"It will have to do."

She simply shook her head and turned away.

"We have to change at this intersection," she said, after a few moments, "if we are going to the jackpole."

"I know."

We transferred to the other belt, and the traffic was somewhat heavier. I was unable to tell whether we were being followed at that time.

"I imagine you are now trying to figure the best way to get rid of me."

"That is correct."

"Give up," she said. "I am not going to go away."

"You have no knowledge of the situation into which you are trying to force your way," I said, "and I am not about to enlighten you. I have already told you that it is dangerous. Anyone who rushes toward an unknown peril simply to satisfy a desire for excitement is a fool. I begin to understand why you cannot hold a job."

"You cannot insult me into going away."

"You *are* a fool!"

"Have it your way," she said, "but I have a right to use public transportation the same as anyone else. I have already decided where I am going, so you might as well be graceful about it."

"It strikes me as in a category with accident-watching."

"My intention is to do more than watch, if necessary."

"I shan't argue with you any further," I said. "But how do you know I am not depraved, psychotic, criminal or any of a number of other undesirable things?"

"It does not matter," she said, "since I have already chosen sides."

"That says something about your own stability."

"I suppose it does. But why should it matter to you, if I don't mind your being all those things?"

"Never mind. Forget it."

I watched the jackpole for a time. Overhead, a crane ground by, bearing a massive load of office furniture. In a pit to our right, the darkness was smeared away by the bright tongue of a welder, repairing or replacing a conduit. Faintly, very faintly, and but briefly, I heard some strains of music. Far ahead now, a geometrically

78

disciplined parklike area came into view at the base of the jackpole. It was not overly lit, there was a statue of somebody or other at the near end and benches here and there along the walks. As we drew nearer, I saw that the trees were natural, not artificial, and there seemed to be a fountain toward the rear.

"It reminds me of something out of Wolfe," Glenda said, looking in the same direction, and I became more Hinkley than anything else, almost without realizing it.

"Yes," I found myself saying. "He got a lot of mileage out of the town square, didn't he?"

"This one could use a city hall and a courthouse with a big clock on it."

"There is a clock above the entrance to the jackpole."

"Yes, but it is silent and always has the right time."

"That's true. No bird droppings either."

"Could use a stonemason's shop, too."

"But not the tombstones."

"True."

I wondered then about real squares back on the Earth. Did the strange Mr. Black really remember such things, or had he simply been killing time before he killed me? Since I had no such recollections on which to base any nostalgia, I could only blame my feelings on Hinkley's preoccupations: he was a romantic, an armchair time-traveler, a naturalist in a place that was all out of nature. Sad. And that was how I felt for several moments. About Hinkley, squares, everything.

"You read a lot," I said.

She nodded.

We disembarked at the park and walked into it. Periodically, hidden speakers released recorded bird-notes from within the bushes and trees. The peculiar smell of moist earth came to our nostrils. I directed our route around the jackpole, where we passed beside the small, sparkling fountain. Glenda dipped her fingers.

"What are we doing?" she asked, as we completed our circuit of the pole and headed back in the direction from which we had come.

"Biding a bit," I said, as I eased myself onto a bench and stared back along the walk toward the beltway.

She settled herself beside me, followed the direction of my gaze.

"I see," she said.

"While we are biding, you might tell me something about yourself," I said.

"What do you want to know?"

"Anything. Free-associate for me."

"Will you return the favor?"

"Maybe. Why? Is that a condition?"

"It would be nice."

"I will see what I can think of to say while you are talking."

"I am twenty-two years old," she said. "I was born in this Wing. I grew up in the Classroom. My father was a teacher and my mother was an artist—a painter. They are both dead now, and I live in the Library. I—"

I gripped her arm.

"That's him?" she said, studying the figure which had just come into view on the beltway. "The enemy you flee?"

"I cannot be sure," I said. "But I am going to operate under the assumption that it is. Come on."

We returned to the far side of the pole and entered there.

"You could just be doing this to keep from talking about yourself," she said.

"I could, but I am not."

We began the descent, augmenting our speed by walking rapidly down the gyre. Running to get away, then waiting for the pursuit to catch up could prove self-defeating if I continued the practice any further. It was not my intention, however. I had wanted to establish something, and I believed that I just had.

If it were the same man, it seemed to me that he would have been following at too great a distance to maintain visual contact for the whole junket from the Living Room. While he might be good at anticipating me, the ability was hardly a thing in which to invest complete confidence. Since his hand had already been exposed and it seemed fairly certain that he was out for blood, it would seem to follow that he had some means of tracking me which I had not so far considered.

How could he have planted a transmitter on me?

The answer was not long in coming, although it was of no immediate use. My present clothing had hung in a locker, unattended, while I was on the bandstand. It would not have been overly difficult to get to it and insert something that would broadcast my whereabouts when I left.

It could be microscopic, though, and situated anywhere. Locating it could be quite an undertaking. Unfortunately, the alternative of discarding my garments would not serve to make me less conspicuous in this Wing.

I was glad that I had taken the time to test him though. If I had not, I would be leading him toward my jumping-off place, even if I appeared to lose him. That would never do.

We rode all the way down, to the Basement, and my plan was already in pretty good focus by the time we reached it.

Save for maintenance people, the Basement was pretty much unfrequented. But it was a wilderness of machinery—reactors, generators, circulators, conditioners, pumps, computers, transformers, indicator panels—half-hidden in a jungle of pipes and cables, service belts every few yards, metal stairways that seemed to lead nowhere, flimsy platforms that vibrated when you mounted them, a maze of catwalks at every level, gantries, cranes, the smells of grease and burnt insulation, an unremitting hum, rush, whirr and crackle arising from it and the blue presence of electricity everywhere.

... All of which offered plenty of physical cover, as well as possible interference for whatever broadcast device I might be wearing.

I stood for a moment and took my bearings. Although I could make out a couple of distant jackpoles, it was a subway exchange that I wanted. I located signs indicating the way to the nearest and headed toward the belt leading in that direction. My intention was to skip from Wing to Wing until I hit a station offering immediate transport to the Room I wanted, whatever the Wing, and then move directly to Go, without stopping, without collecting two hundred dollars, cursing the whole damned game the while. If my man could track me through interstellar space perhaps he deserved to win. I had strong doubts concerning his capability along these lines, however.

... And somewhere, before I reached the Gate, I would have to dispose of Glenda. I could not very well take her along to the place where I was going, and I saw no real danger to her should I leave her behind. A quick shot of trank as soon as I was certain we were alone, and she could sleep this one out on some workman's bench. It would be safer for her than keeping her with me much longer, I decided.

It was a wide belt and it was slow, but it had us out of sight of the jackpole within a minute, so packed were the environs with the equipment that maintained the Wing. Once we were in the midst of it, we felt rather than heard the throb of the place. Two quick changeovers and we were on a narrower, faster belt, the course of which roughly paralleled the first. We were actually only a few hundred feet away from it, but it was completely hidden to us. So far, we had encountered no other people.

Anyone descending the jackpole might still catch sight of us without our seeing him, though, because of the way the lights played on the surface of the thing. If someone was, he might have seen me shrug at the thought, because that was about all I was able to do for the moment.

I wondered about the others—what they were thinking, doing, whether they had guessed my present situation correctly. This seemed likely, since they knew I was alive and therefore doubtless aware of the most recent killings, yet had no new orders for them. They must have guessed that I was still running and would contact them as soon as I could, that attempts to contact me could only distract me from my immediate problems. I wondered how much initiative they possessed. We would have to confer again as soon as I reached Wing Null.

We walked quickly, adding our own speed to that of the belt. The light was very bright, almost glaring, for it was always full day here. Cranes moved constantly overhead, dipping, rising, sidling. The machinery hissed, chattered, hummed, hissed, chattered, hummed. I felt an irrational relief when we passed a callbox and the phone within it did not jangle.

"Will you tell me now why you are fleeing, and from whom?" Glenda said.

"No."

"It might be helpful if I knew."

"You invited yourself on this trip," I said. "It is not a conducted tour."

"The danger I felt earlier . . . it is very near now."

82

"I hope that you are wrong."

But I felt that she was right. My paranoid tendencies were easily stimulated, but they had had a lot of practice recently. I took the next sidebelt to my right, not knowing where it headed. Dutifully, she followed. We were squeezed between towering cliffs of metal. The temperature soared, quickly became oppressive. About twenty feet overhead, two workmen on a metal scaffold stared down at us with something of surprise on their faces.

We took several more turnings, even spending a couple of minutes on a maintenance belt so narrow we had to stand sideways. After a time, we found our way to another, more normal belt, heading in the proper direction. The only other people we passed were schoolchildren on a tour of the ventilation complex. They were far off to our left, and quickly lost to sight.

I began looking about for a safe nook or cranny in which to leave Glenda. I drew my gun and palmed it. I did feel a certain uneasiness at the thought. I do not like leaving loose ends about, I guess that was it. I was curious about her. A strange girl, who could not hold a job, who had helped me . . . I would check back on her as soon as possible. I would attend to her welfare as soon as I had assured my own.

". . . Don't look suddenly," I heard her saying, "but I think we *are* being followed. Not on the belt. Up above. To the left. Back."

I turned my head, trying to be casual about it. One brief glance was sufficient, and I looked away again.

He was up on the catwalks, moving at a brisk pace, shortcutting us, gaining.

. . . And those bright, bright lights shone upon the blue of his glasses.

I saved my curses. I had more than half expected him. For a pathological instant, I wished that I were bearing something more potent than a tranquilizer gun. I pushed the thought aside. I took two paces forward, and Glenda immediately followed.

"Damn it! Don't stand so close to me!" I said.

"It may be to your advantage that I do."

"And your disadvantage. Stay away!"

"In a word: No."

83

"All right. I have warned you. That is all I can do. Enjoy your excitement."

"I am."

My mind raced ahead. I had been faster than Lange, but perhaps still not fast enough. If not, so be it. Maybe I deserved to die. The fact that I was stronger than Lange had been by himself was no assurance that I was fit enough to survive the present situation. I had at least learned a few things about my pursuer and I intended to learn a few more.

I checked ahead, seeking some hunk of machinery with crawlspaces, slots, overhangs—a place where I would be a difficult target, but could get off some clear shots myself. Several possibles presented themselves. Then I looked back, trying to estimate his rate of progress.

"What are you going to do?" Glenda asked me.

I was beginning to have a funny feeling which I could not quite explain, but I had no time to analyze it.

"Bleed all over you," I said, "unless you do exactly what I tell you."

"I am listening."

"Ahead. To the right. About three hundred yards ... The big gray machine with the black cowl on the near end. See it?"

"Yes. It's a Langton generator."

"I am going to head to the left in about a minute. When I do, you remain on the belt for a few more seconds. He will be watching me. Then you will be almost abreast of that thing. Run for it and get in behind it. As soon as I occupy that man overhead, back off and lose yourself in the complex to the rear. Keep an eye on what happens and gauge your actions accordingly. Good luck."

"No. I'm coming with you."

Turning my body so that it could not be seen from behind and above, I twisted my hand and pointed the gun.

"If you try it, I'll trank you and let the belt take you out of here. Don't argue. Do as I say."

Then I jumped down and dashed for the refuge I had chosen, catching sight of the figure overhead as he hurried toward me, his right arm rising.

I heard the shot. With him running like that and all, I was not surprised that he missed. I was out of his line of sight before he got off another. I scrambled around the corner of the unit and moved into the channel I had seen, which cut partway through its middle, was interrupted by a three-foot-high hedge of metal and some hanging cables, then seemed to continue unobstructed to its farther end. There appeared to be eight service adits along its way, and a possible side channel. I could see upward through the gaps among struts and cables, and it pleased me that I had guessed correctly: He would have to get awfully close in order to fire successfully through that mess.

I was only a few paces into it when I heard her.

"Damn!" I said, turning. "I told you to head for the generator!"

"I decided not to," she said. "I knew you would not look back once you began running."

I shrugged, turned away and continued forward. I heard her following. I could see several sections of the catwalk, including a branch that passed above the far end of the machine. According to my calculations, he could be coming into sight any moment now.

"What should I do to help?" I heard Glenda say.

"Whatever strikes your fancy," I said. "I resign all responsibility for your welfare. Your death is on your own head."

I heard a sharp intake of breath and she bit off the beginning of something she had begun to say. I continued to edge forward.

He could have descended one of the ladders or walkways to the floor and be working his way toward us through the mazes of hardware. Or he could be halted or proceeding along another overhead route. He might be very near. It was futile to listen for footfalls, because of the background noise, because of the vibrations of the machine within which we stood.

As I drew near the possible side channel, however, a sharp sound did succeed in penetrating everything. It was the ringing of a telephone in some service niche nearby.

Cursing under my breath and flattening myself against the wall, I resolved to introduce the thing into his alimentary canal from one end or the other at my first opportunity. This time, however, I remained steady. The sound played hell with my nerves, but I succeeded in maintaining control.

A moment later, I heard the crash of his boots and realized what he had done.

Somehow aware of the manner in which the ringing would affect me, he obviously carried a repairman's service unit capable of locating and activating phones. He had worked his way to a position above my shelter, buzzed the nearest call box in hope of disconcerting me, and dropped down atop the machine. Only this time I was not biting. Pressing against the housing, I could feel rather than hear his quick steps. He was seeking an opening, looking for a clear shot. Hoping to find me a quivering mass of jelly, I presumed.

Suddenly, a head, arm and shoulder flashed into view, high up, to my right, about thirty feet down the channel, from behind a juncture of beams.

Even as I whipped my own weapon upward and squeezed, I heard the sound of his shot and the sound of its ricochet. Then he was gone.

I backed up. I bumped into Glenda. Without looking, I pushed her toward the niche, snarling something unintelligible and backing in myself. As I crowded back against her, I heard the thud of his boots again and realized that he had leaped across the right-hand channel. I moved my gun to cover what I guessed to be his new position and felt a sudden, insane pleasure at the thought that the phone had stopped ringing.

Then he appeared, fired again, missed. I got off another shot, too. The next time, I felt, would decide it. He knew my position now.

I leaned back and aimed upward. It was going to be over the top of the niche this time, I felt it.

My chances, as I saw them, were not good. Even if I nailed him perfectly, he was going to get off a shot. My concern, along with protecting the girl, centered upon the seriousness of the injuries I would sustain, should I survive. I was going to get him—I knew it, I felt it, I swore it. Even if he put that bullet right through my heart again, my reflexes would snap off a shot and he would be out for a while, up there. I wanted to live, to drag him back to Wing Null with me, to turn his mind inside out and dump its contents on the floor. It would be so wasteful, to die, to leave him vulnerable and not be able to do anything about it.

"... If I die," I heard myself saying to Glenda, "and leave him unconscious up there," and it was not me that was saying the terrible thing I overheard, I realized, even though the words were coming from my own mouth, "would you be willing to go up and finish him off with his own gun? A bullet through the brain? The heart?"

"No! I couldn't! I wouldn't!"

"It would save me a lot of trouble later."

"Later?" She giggled, half-hysterically. "If you're dead—" Then she shut up, but I could feel her heavy breathing, her tenseness.

What was he waiting for? Damn him!

"Come on!" I cried. "This is the last time! Even if you get me, you're dead!"

Nothing. Still nothing.

Then I heard Glenda whispering, rapidly, urgently.

"You are the one. I was right. Listen. It is important. Take me with you to the secret place. I have something for you. It is important—"

It was also too late. There were three more footfalls and a thud, as he leaped across our channel and fired downward. I felt a searing pain down my chest and ribcage. I fired back, felt that I had hit him.

White pants, blue jacket, long brown hair, blue mirror-glasses, he had turned as he jumped, landed in a half-crouched position, left arm thrown high for balance, right extended downward, weapon pointed, clenched teeth showing through a tight, humorless smile.

"Mr. Black! No!" I heard Glenda scream, as another shot caught me in the shoulder, slamming me back against her.

The trank gun fell from my hand as my whole right arm became useless. I had hit him, though, I knew that.

And it was Mr. Black. It was the same man with whom I had sat in the Cocktail Lounge—how long ago? Eliminating the color and length of hair, the different outfit, the glasses, I saw the same jawline, the same ridges and creases ...

I raised my left hand as he tried to steady his weapon for another shot. Glenda was still screaming as I bit my thumb and glared at him and heard and felt his final shot tear into my guts.

He fell backward then as I toppled forward, a cloud of ink seeming to rise from my middle and rush to my head.

The ringing echo of the shot faded, was gone, though I still felt the vibrations of the machine through the wetness, forming and re-forming the words *Pull pin seven*, and Glenda was crying, "Library! Cubicle 18237! Important! Library! Cubicle 18237 . . ."

Then soft nothing.

4

I picked myself up and started running again. Crazy, but I could not help it.

Good thing that nobody I could see was in any condition to notice.

Then a knot of live ones appeared, and it was either slow down or become conspicuous—the last thing I wanted to do. I bit my lip, looked in all directions, came to a halt, took several deep breaths.

Then something of Engel began to take hold, and it was better . . .

Tough. Who would have thought Engel able to acquit himself as well as he had? An aging clarinetist—a quiet, peaceable guy. Now only I/he/we knew what had been inside him, and I already different, never to be quite the same again, still changing, aware of the process like mercury within me, impossible to pin down, heavy, flashing, flowing, providing strength, steadiness . . .

Tough, we were tougher than I had thought. It was just that the engine had had to cough a few times before it began to function smoothly. We were almost to our goal now and I, Paul Karab, was nexus . . .

My flight had begun as a thing unrecommended and perhaps slightly ignoble, but now it had become a mission. I had done the proper thing for the wrong reasons.

. . . Paul Karab, reasonably healthy, thirty-five-year-old Living Room Representative, Wing 1, youngest member of the Household Staff, running scared.

Now the fright-factor had diminished considerably—just now—now that Engel/Lange was here. Better and better by the moment.

All of the killings had panicked me, each more than the previous. I had passed out on each occasion and come around in worse shape than before. I had been ready to start running at the time of the meshing, but it had served to stabilize me. Then when Serafis and Davis got it, reason had gone up in smoke. I felt that even my position, with all its safeguards, was not proof against this sort of an attack, an attack that was obviously a well-planned attempt to destroy the entire family. I had not possessed curiosity such as Lange had known, nor anger like Engel's. These would have come later, I was certain, but my panic had submerged these important survival factors. I was ashamed of it, but only for a moment. It had served a useful purpose, and I was no longer the person it had overwhelmed.

I watched the slow progress of the mourners following the box on the belt. The preacher walked at their head, pacing the coffin, reading the final prayers. From where I stood, I could see the area where the service had been conducted, but various partitions and furnishings prevented my viewing the black door toward which they were headed. The obvious analogy came and nested in my mind with small clucking sounds, dark feathers and haste: The Paul Karab I had known all my life was dead, half the family was dead, our whole way of life might well be sucking its final breaths.

No.

I would not permit it.

My determination surprised me, but there it was. I knew what I was going to do, had to do. Without having made a conscious decision, I just knew. The others might not approve. But then again, considering the circumstances, they might. Anyway, it was my choice to make.

The Chapel was, as always, a checkerboard of light and darkness. I moved diagonally to my left, passing to the entrance-point to a darkened section. Glancing about, I dropped to the floor and crawled in, not wanting to break the warning beam that would turn on gentle illumination, the odor of incense, relaxing music and lights on the altar. I slipped into a pew and sat sideways, so that I could look back out and keep an eye on the funeral procession. I wanted a cigarette but felt kind of funny about lighting one in there, so I didn't.

From where I was seated, I could see the black door—gateway to eternity, the underworld, the afterlife, whatever. The belt terminated right before the door, feeding back down around its rollers there. As the mourners advanced, tight-faced, dark-clad, slow, a representative of the funeral director moved forward and pressed out an opening sequence on the plate set into that dark frame.

Silently, the door swung inward and the casket passed through it, followed by considerable remembrances of artificial flowers—of course I could not be certain of this from where I sat, but that many real flowers would have cost a fortune, a circumstance denied by the smallness of the cortege—and since the track then inclined at an appropriate downward angle and was equipped with rollers, the entire display vanished smoothly from sight. Then the door closed, there were some final words from the clerical-type and the people turned and slowly moved away, talking among themselves or silent, as things had it.

I watched them go, waited perhaps ten minutes until the area went dim, waited ten more. Then I rose, crossed over, crawled out again.

Still, silent . . . Even the pall-belt had been turned off. The nearest illuminated area was a good distance away, far enough so that I could not even hear the music.

I advanced, moved up to the belt. For some reason, I reached out and touched it, trailing my hand along it as I walked beside it toward the wall. Tactile person? I thought of Glenda. What was she doing right now? Where was she? Had she contacted the police, or simply fled? Steady finally, my thoughts moved back to those final moments which they had, till now, but skirted. What had she been saying right there at the end? Not the usual hysterical nonsense one would expect from a young woman in the presence of sudden, violent death. No, it had not seemed that way. She had been repeating an address and telling me how important it was. If this were not a form of hysteria, though, the alternative was disconcerting. What use could a dying man have for the information, unless he happened to be me?

But she could not have known. There was no way I could think of for her to have known.

. . . Or anyone else, for that matter. Say, Mr. Black.

. . . Whom she apparently recognized.

Going back a bit further, it was somewhat unusual, our meeting the way that we had . . .

I would have to find out, of course. Anything that might have some bearing on the present unpleasantness was vital.

. . . And her seeming irrational insistence on accompanying me.

Yes, I would have to pursue the matter. Quite soon.

I crossed over the belt, moved parallel to it, approached the black door. I had to be on the right side in order to reach the plate.

I halted when I came to the black door, the route by which the dead depart the House, the only way anyone leaves the House. It was of a light alloy, was about six feet by eight and in the dim light seemed more a blot or a hole than an object. I manipulated the plate and it swung silently inward. More blackness. Even standing where I was, it was difficult to tell that it was now open. Which suited me fine.

I mounted the belt and stepped through, leaning to the rear to maintain my balance and keeping one hand on the smooth wall. I caught hold of the door then and drew it toward me, pivoting about its advancing edge, and pushed it closed. It would not snap true until I activated the mechanism, but it would do if someone came along during the next few minutes.

I got down on all fours again and crawled backward down the tunnel. It only runs about forty feet. When I reached the rear wall, I rose, leaning against it, and slid my fingers along its surface, seeking the maintenance box.

It took only a moment to locate it and slide its coverplate open. When I did, its small interior light came on and I could see what I was doing once again. The unit seldom, if ever, required servicing, and what I did to it then was definitely not in the service manual. There was no reason, anyway, for anyone to fool with the broadcast coordinates that sent the dead on their one-way subway ride among the stars.

No one but one of us, that is.

I finished, slid the panel shut and waited. There would be a lapse of fifteen seconds before it functioned. After that, it would reset itself to its old coordinates.

Somewhere behind and above me, I heard the door click faintly. All right. There was something I was supposed to remember . . .

I was suddenly pitched to the ground. I caught myself with my hands, slipped onto my side and rose to my feet again. Yes, I was supposed to remember that while I was standing on an incline in the tunnel, the surface to which I was transferring was not so canted.

Then there was light all about me. It was a brief, bright corridor, the walls so brilliant and dazzling that they hurt my eyes. As I shielded my gaze and moved along it, my person was being analyzed at hundreds—perhaps thousands—of levels, by hidden devices which would only permit one person to pass through the door at its end.

As I neared it, the door slid upward, and I echoed its sigh as I passed through and into Wing Null.

The feeling of relief, of release, was intense and immediate. I had come home. I was safe. The enemy could not reach me here.

I followed the curving of the red-carpeted hallway to the left, moving about the hub of the fortress, passing the great sealed vaults of Lab, Comp, Storage and Files. I wondered as I walked concerning the state of mind that had moved some earlier version of myself to give them such prosaic names, considering what they really held. Sardonic, I guess.

I continued on by them all and entered the study or lounge that eventually occurred on my right. The lights came on as I did so and I extinguished them with a slap, the illumination from the hallway being sufficient. It was a small room, light-walled, dark-carpeted, containing a desk, two easy chairs, a couch with end tables, a glassed-in bookcase. Everything was just as I remembered it.

I crossed over to the far, blank wall, switched on the control in the chair rail and transpared it.

It was night outside, and a fat, orange moon hung above the white, stone hills about half a mile to my left, giving them the appearance of half a jawbone filled with fractured teeth. Near to hand, the rocks were dark and slick, giving the appearance of having been rained upon recently. There was a flock of pale, retreating clouds in the distance and a bright profusion of stars overhead. An indicator off to my right showed me that the temperature out there was a little over 13° C. I backed away, turned an easy chair to face the panorama and seated myself.

Still staring, I located a cigarette, lit it, smoked.

No matter how urgent the situation was, I had to have this moment, this cigarette, this view of the outside, before I took the next step. I had to be in a tranquil state of mind before I could proceed. It would make a difference.

What it came down to was that I was going to have to violate several directives in order to follow another one. It was a matter of judgment. If we were to mesh now, I believed there would be considerable disagreement, but I was the nexus, the sole heir to Engel's final experiences and the only one in a position to take action. The decision was mine to make and I had made it.

Bravo! We finally have someone with some sense in the driver's seat!

"It was none of it your doing, old-timer," I said.

Of course it was! All the way!

"Well, I am not about to argue with you over it. It makes little difference now, and will make none whatsoever in a short while."

Perhaps.

"What do you mean 'perhaps'?"

Let us wait and see—in a short while.

"You have no better idea of what will happen than I do. Well, not much better."

I suppose you are right. Shall we go and find out?

"You have waited this long. You can damned well wait until I finish my cigarette."

All right. Enjoy your brooding. You don't even understand what you are looking at.

"I suppose you do?"

Better than you.

"We'll see."

We will.

The night was sufficiently illuminated for me to make out several large craters in the distance, their outlines softened by a low growth of dark vegetation. Staring hard, I could also discern the outlines of the great, ruined, fortresslike building at the foot of the hills. The prospect fascinated me. Maybe I was going to learn some more about it . . .

Enough! There were so many things! That ruin . . . How many hundreds of times had I seen it? Through how many eyes?

Rising, I mashed out my cigarette in a nearby tray, turned, and left the room.

My excitement was high by the time I reached the Files vault. I commenced the delicate, complicated and potentially fatal manipulations of its lock mechanism.

A quarter of an hour later, I had it open. I entered and the lights came on. Several moments later, the door closed and relocked itself behind me.

The room ran back about forty feet at the middle and was around sixty across. Its rear wall was concave, curving about the operating area, which was raised a foot or so above the floor. A lap-level countertop ran along the entire wall, extending out for perhaps thirty inches. Mounted above it were bank upon bank of control assemblies, sweeping outward like wings from the central board and its console. The massive control chair was swiveled in my direction, as if waiting.

I took off my jacket as I walked forward, folded it, placed it on a shelf. Then I seated myself, turned to the console and began warming the thing up. It took about ten minutes to ready it, what with checking out systems and activating subunits in their proper sequence. I was glad of this, for the activity fully occupied my attention for a time.

Finally, though, the lights were arrayed in the proper order, and it was time to begin.

I opened the cabinet to my left, swung out the hood on its long, heavy arm. I ran several quick checks on it, also. Perfect.

I fitted it over my head, lowering it until it rested upon my shoulders. There was an opening about the eyes which permitted me to see what I was doing. I activated the mechanism which caused it to check me out.

There was a vibration as its innards rotated to align themselves with whatever they deemed salient portions of my cranial anatomy. Then there came a tightening as pads moved into place against my skull. There followed a small jolt and a few traces of moisture. The anesthetic. As it was vibrated through the skin, some of it was blocked by my hair. That was all right, though. I did not want to shave or wear a wig. I could stand a little runoff down my neck.

I do not suppose that anyone enjoys contemplating the

violation of his innards, least of all the interior of his skull. Whatever one's knowledge and experience, thinking about feelings gives rise to emotions. It need not even be necessary that the feelings actually occur. Within a very brief span, however, the blue indicator flashed before me and I realized that all of the necessary filaments had succeeded in painlessly penetrating my scalp, skull, dura, arachnoid and pia mater, worked their ways into appropriate areas of my brain and formed themselves into a network capable of performing the work they had to do. And I was still gnawing my lower lip. Thus are we hoist by our own forebrain.

The machinery was ready. Now was the time for the standard procedure employed by each new nexus. Now was the time for me to go back through my/our/the mind and systematically erase all those portions of Lange and Engel which I felt to be in conflict with my own personality and to excise their memories dealing with things before my own time. Now was the time for the sacrifice, the partial suicide, the jettisoning of the excess baggage, of the things which served only to clutter the mind, create conflicts, make life less tolerable. As no one knows how much the human mind can hold, somewhere along the line we decided not to tamper with its limits. I believed that to be the reason. Somewhere, back in the dreamtime, the decision was made. To the best of my knowledge, we had always proceeded on the basis of this rationale, and since the family was still around, it had always proved effective. Until now, of course. Now was the time for Lange and Engel to depart—to become, perhaps, autonomous complexes, or personal demons in the underworld of my subconscious.

Now, however, the threat to our existence was foremost in my mind, and I wanted to be larger, not smaller, to know more things, not fewer. Preserved in memory and ringed round with a directive not to erase, was the notion that, as an emergency procedure in a time of great peril, the dead might be resurrected. I did not believe it had ever been employed, and of course had no idea what the result might be. That it would be more than memory, though, was obvious. Still, I felt myself a very definite and very real me, despite being partly Lange and partly Engel. The situation warranted drastic action.

96

I became very conscious of my heartbeat as I turned my attention to the patchboard with its seven pins and spaces for many more.

Each pin, the life of a nexus; each, a generation of our kind skewered there like an invisible butterfly . . .

My palm was moist as I reached forward.

A pin was inserted in the master board each time the process of erasure was completed. To draw one would be to undo the work of a predecessor, to cause *his* predecessor to live again within me.

What was I doing? I was supposed to be here to insert pin eight . . .

My hand began to shake.

This was wrong! It was ridiculous even to consider . . .

My hand grew steady, continued to move forward. I tried, but was unable to halt it.

I watched with a peculiar fascination, as it moved across the board, settled upon its target and withdrew pin seven.

5

I was not at all certain what it was I had expected. A clash of cymbals? A mind-riving jolt, followed by unconsciousness? Something dramatic, I guess.

It was, however, more than anything else, like waking up in the morning, memories of the previous day gradually hefting themselves above the horizon. A mere clearing of the head, revealing what had been there all along. A gallery of familiar pictures.

Old Lange . . .

Of course. It had been an instance where we had posed as being our own son. It was only chance that the nexus passed from one Lange-identity to another. And there had been others in the mesh, long forgotten, but with me once again, as if they had never been away.

I was now the demon who had been addressing us. I was Engel, Lange, Lange Senior and those things the older Lange had retained of his predecessor, a strange mind I would almost have called alien minutes earlier: Winton. But regarding him as his successor had seen fit to preserve him, he did not seem all that different. What was it? What was happening? My accumulated memories now ran back for over a century, but it was more than a matter of timespan and quantity. The sense of differentness that accompanied the reavailability of all this experience was . . . qualitative. Yes, that was it. And what was the quality?

That is something you cannot truly appreciate in your present state.

Powerful. There. Him. Winton. For a moment, I was too dumbstruck to reply. The knowledge had always been present, but I had not taken the time to consider it—that in releasing Lange's demon and absorbing him, I would come up against the older, earlier interface, with the demon of whom I had previously known nothing capable of addressing me from behind it.

You needed what you have now, he was saying, *as a point of departure. You are smarter and somewhat stronger for what you have obtained, but it is not sufficient against Mr. Black. To understand, and to possess the ability to do something about it will require the pulling of pin six. Do it now.*

Determined. And strong. He was. In his insistence. That was what made the decision for me. I wanted that determination, that strength.

That is why, before I could marshal the arguments against it, I moved my hand several inches upward on a diagonal and pulled pin six.

Yes! Yes, as the fogs rolled away and my memory reached back for perhaps a century and a half, it was not only the recalling of vast quantities of experience that moved me. The memories themselves, still, were dreamlike and not especially charged with emotion. It was a tightening, a toughening of attitude that came into me, that reassured me as to my own ability to deal with the present situation. And more, more than that . . .

I had hardly begun sorting out my reactions, let alone considering the matter which had elicited them, when Birnam Wood began to shuffle its feet, so to speak.

The feeling. God, the feeling . . . It was like flood waters suddenly welling behind an ancient dam. I felt the gathering might, I was uncertain as to the fortifications.

Yes, you were weak and you have been strengthened. But now is not the time to stop. Reach out and take it all. You need every weapon you can get your hands on right now. You will face an enemy who is also strong. For this reason you must be more fully yourself. Pull pin five and restore me within you. I will show you how to deal with Mr. Black.

"No," I said. "Wait," I said. "Wait . . ."

There is no time. Black's position grows stronger with every moment you delay. Do not discard the tool that may cut the diamond, throw away the stone that may be key to the arch. You will need me. Pull pin five!

My hand moved toward it, but I feared I might have gone too far already. There was no way to gauge the strength of the entity that would then urge me to pull pin four, and then three—and all the way back, to the beginning, unbuilding the painfully erected edifice, undoing centuries of collective effort to achieve moral evolution.

I share your sentiments, I agree with your principles. They are all of them useless, however, if you are no longer available to further them. You require my knowledge of specifics in order to defend yourself properly. Therefore, as the day the night ... Pull pin five! Now!

The muscles in my arm began to ache. My fingers were curved and stiff, clawlike.

"No!" I said. "Damn it! No!"

You must!

My hand jerked, my fingertips touched the pin.

I had gone too far too fast. I was way off balance in every department of my mind. He might be right, Jordan—I suddenly knew that to be his name. He might be right. But I was not going to have him pressure me into it. I was not even certain what I had just become. To release another unknown within myself was tantamount to lunacy.

Of course you are uncertain. But you must also realize that your hesitancy jeopardizes the others, as well as the girl ...

"Wait!"

Then the anger came, deadly. I, James Winton, had blotted him out, sacrificed him, broken him with my will. Now this pitiful ragtag, tail-end self was trying to order me about!

Slowly, I clenched my right hand into a fist. Then I slammed it down against the countertop.

"No!" I said. "I have what I need."

You are a fool!

I raised my hand, very deliberately, and pressed my thumb against pin five.

Silence.

Trying not to think of anything, not to sort out any thoughts or feelings, I shifted to a motor level of activity and began the process of disengaging myself from the equipment.

Finally, the pressure let up on my head and the lights indicated that the hood might be removed. I did this, returning it to its cabinet, then shut down all units and departed Files, sealing the place carefully behind me. I moved along the hallway to Comp and began the unlocking procedure there. Then I returned to my den, for the time-lock mechanism on Comp had a little over ten minutes to go.

I flopped into the chair, lit another cigarette and stared out into the night. The moon had traveled a detectable distance in the brief while I had been away. The shadow patterns had shifted across the landscape, revealing more evidence of ancient devastation as well as additional vegetation. The prospect was considerably more familiar to me now than it had been earlier, though I still did not understand the nature of the carnage. A war, perhaps? There was something even more intriguing and disturbing about the ruins at the foot of those stark hills now . . .

My ruminations were cut short as I stared at that wreckage. It seemed as though there had been a movement.

I rose and crossed to the window.

Again, something. A glint . . . Yes, there was a flicker of light back within the collapsed walls. I continued to watch, and it came again, several times. I tried timing the flashes, but there did not seem to be any special pattern to them.

Then there was a blaze, as though a beacon had been swung quickly across the wracked landscape and fallen directly upon me, where it stopped.

I raised my arm to shield my eyes against its brilliance, and with my other hand I felt for the control and darkened the window once more.

I sank back into the chair then, some small part of me surprised that I was not especially disconcerted by the phenomenon. The feeling quickly passed. Nothing that strange about the light, really. It had undergone periodic bursts of such activity for generations. I had just forgotten—or, rather, just remembered—about it. Yes, it seemed something mechanical that was occasionally disturbed, underwent a brief spasm of activity, lapsed into quiescence again. One of the *so what?* facts of existence.

Or was it? Oh, hell! I had more pressing matters demanding my attention.

Like, who was I? I realized I was no longer the same individual who had come to Wing Null. And it was not a loss, but a gain. That was the way I felt about it. But what was the gain?

101

I felt more Winton than Karab, to be truthful about it. But it was as if this had always, really, been so, and the other was but a temporary phase, a life-laboratory I had employed for the conduct of certain experiments. And the necessity was now upon me to abandon this research for a time, in order to deal with larger matters which had arisen to trouble me.

Lord! how naive I had allowed myself to become! I smiled at my prissy latterday selves. Their fears. Their qualms.

On whose shoulders did they think they stood? Who had bought them the right to indulge their precious squeamishness? Who had provided the opportunity for them to exercise their higher instincts, as a band of anonymous humanitarians and benefactors of the House? Within the present generation, the time of Lange, they had stopped a plague, prevented several large-scale disasters from being far worse than they were, promoted several productive lines of medical research, discouraged three programs of scientific inquiry which could have led in an undesirable direction, guided the computers and politicians toward several sound decisions concerning population control, aggression-surrogation and areas of emphasis in education, aided in the development of new amusements, saw the crime rate decline even further and assisted numerous groups and individuals in times of distress. But why had they had this opportunity to indulge in what, to some, might seem officious intermeddling, to others, altruism? Their way had been paved with thought, sweat, sacrifice and more than a little blood.

On the other hand, it had all been worth it. Strange, to think of myself simultaneously from two temporal perspectives. But they were merging, merging even as I thought them, and I felt considerably enriched therefor. Jordan's perspective would be even broader, I knew. I had some of his memories, and I knew that he went back a long while. Perhaps I had been hasty in dealing with him—

No! The line had to be drawn somewhere. What I now possessed seemed sufficient. There was a solid, important reason for everything that we did, I knew that. I did not need all of the specifics. Based on my present knowledge of myself, I had faith in all my earlier decisions. I believed

102

that I had never suppressed arbitrarily, that there was a reason for each partial suicide. To undo everything as an exercise in academic curiosity would be an act of madness.

My scalp began to tingle, bringing my thoughts back to more immediate considerations.

I got to my feet. The lock on Comp should be about ready for further manipulation. I massaged my head lightly as I headed back down the hall. I wondered about Gene, Jenkins and Winkel. They were still alive, which was all that really mattered. They should not be in any immediate jeopardy, since I had left Mr. Black somewhat distraught; and they had all had what seemed sufficient time in which to prime their senses of survival and throw up a few defenses. I saw no point in contacting them until I had something to tell them, which would not be for a little while yet.

I had a brief wait remaining before I could get into Comp, which time I spent puzzling over Glenda. It was fairly apparent from her parting comments that she knew something about me. What she knew was not nearly so important to me as how she had come to learn it. And she knew something about my old enemy, who was calling himself Mr. Black these days. If for no other reason than this, she would be high on my schedule of priorities.

The mechanism came to its final activation point, I completed the sequence, opened the door and entered. The layout of the room was similar to that of Files, only cast on a somewhat larger scale. Here, too, equipment—though of a different variety—filled the far wall and the control chair, while situated farther to the left, was of the same comfortable order as the other. I locked the door behind me and moved toward it.

I activated the Bandit. Funny, my nickname for the thing had been dropped somewhere along the line, to be replaced by the simple, bland understatement: Comp. It was more than a computing device, however. It was also a data embezzler. The fact that its operations had never been detected was some sort of tribute to the skill of its nameless creator, who had provided it surreptitious access to the master data banks of Wing 1. And more, even more than this. Should necessity require, it could monitor, compute the best points of violation and introduce new materials. Comp, indeed!

So I set it to looking for Mr. Black. My hopes were not great in this department, but I had to try. He might have slipped up somewhere this time around. I had a fairly extensive file on him, already digested within the Bandit's gleaming guts, and it drew on this in its search. A mistake had been made—albeit an understandable one—in eradicating this portion of our memory. The erasure had probably occurred because the whole affair did seem to have been concluded satisfactorily and conscious recall of the violence was an undesirable thing to my carefully civilized scions. That made it my mistake, by proxy, anyway. So I had to be understanding and forgiving, damn it!

I set the Bandit to finding me a history for Glenda, as well as her most recently recorded movements. I also ran vital-statistics searches for Hinkley, Lange, Davis, Serafis and Engel, to see whether any of the deaths had been reported yet.

Then the klaxon began squawking and I was full of adrenalin and on my feet in an instant.

I moved to a sideboard to my left, flicked on a viewscreen and activated an arsenal after switching the many deadlies from automatic to manual control.

I was disappointed when I saw that the arrivals were Winkel and a coffin. A scan showed the mass and indicated the nonliving status of the coffin's contents—so presumably the box contained what was left of Lange. I smiled at my disappointment. I should have been happy that Winkel, of all of us, had proved successful in what he had set out to do. Instead, I was a little irritated that it was not Mr. Black, trying again. He would soon discover that I lacked a few of my brethren's qualms. Among other things, those two pins had represented over a century's inhibitions. So far, he had only had clay pigeons to shoot at. It was about time he encountered a rabid vampire bat. I only hoped that I would have time to tell him it was Winton, again, before the end.

I turned off the klaxon and switched on a speaker.

"Good show, Winkel," I said. "I'll be there to help you in a minute. I'm in Comp."

"Karab," he said, facing the screen, a fairer, thirty-year-old version of myself. "I was worried. When you didn't mesh——"

"Relax. The situation is improving."

I turned off the screen and the speaker, opened a drawer, removed a small pistol, checked it over and loaded it, jammed it into my pocket. Why, I am not certain. Something about the hardiness of old habits, I guess, for it was certainly not that I was unable to trust anyone, even——and I chuckled at the thought——myself.

I departed then, there being no delay in opening the door from the inside, and I felt a small twinge of conscience at not locking it behind me, so deep-dug was the routine's rut. Damn Mr. Black, anyway! He was the reason for the whole procedure, that time he had actually made it to Wing Null and only been surprised by accident. If I had nailed him then, life would be so much simpler.

I moved on up the hall, passed through the entrance defenses and nodded at Winkel, who stood looking tense beside the coffin.

"All right," I said, "let's lug the guts over to Storage. We have a lot of things to do."

He nodded back, and we caught hold of the thing and carried it out.

"I was worried you hadn't made it here," he said as we went.

"Your fears were obviously groundless."

"Yes," he said, and moments later as we deposited the container outside the storage vault and I was turning my attention to the lock, "That looks like a gun in your pocket."

"It is."

"It doesn't look like a trank gun. It looks like one of the other kind."

"That's right."

"What is it for?"

"Think about it for a minute," I said, as I manipulated the locking mechanism.

I worked it to the point where the time device took over, then straightened and jerked my head to the right.

"Come on over to Comp. I have some things to check while we wait."

He followed me, but halted abruptly as we neared the door.

"It isn't locked!" he said.

"True. Time is more than a little essential just now," I replied, pushing it open.

He followed me inside, saying nothing as I crossed to the Bandit to learn the results of my inquiries. As I had suspected, Mr. Black had covered himself well. There was nothing on him, yet. The Bandit would continue its search, of course, looking farther and farther afield for indications of the man.

None of our deaths had been recorded yet, I noted. Probably Hinkley's place was such a mess that they still had not determined who all was involved. And it was kind of soon to have anything in on Engel, even supposing the body had been found—which may not have been the case.

... No indeed, I decided, as I began skimming the data on Glenda. Mr. Black was not about to report it, and the more I learned about Glenda the less predictable she seemed.

"Did you have any trouble getting Lange's body here?" I asked.

"No, no difficulty. No one had come across—"

The klaxon sounded once more. I switched the screen on again and saw that it was Jenkins.

I killed the klaxon, activated the speaker and said, "Hello. Winkel and I are in the Comp Room. Come on over. Don't trip on Lange."

I broke the circuit before he could reply, another nervous youngster of our size and build.

I felt Winkel's gaze and I turned to face him.

"You have changed," he said. "Tremendously. I do not understand what has happened, what is happening. Why didn't you mesh with us after you got here? Why not do it now?"

"Patience," I said. "Right now time is a very expensive commodity and I have to budget it carefully. I will explain everything before too long. Trust me."

He smiled weakly and nodded.

"You do know what to do, then?"

I returned the nod.

"I know what to do."

Moments later, Jenkins arrived. He was breathing heavily and his face was flushed.

106

"What's happening?" he yelled, and he sounded more than a little hysterical. "What's happening?"

Winkel moved to him, seized his shoulder and said, "Take it easy, take it easy. Karab's going to explain everything. He knows how to handle it."

Jenkins shuddered once, then seemed to shrink a little. He turned his head and stared at me.

"I hope so, I really hope you do," he said, regaining control of his voice and softening it, slowing it. "Maybe you can start by telling me what happened to Wing 5."

"What do you mean?" I asked. "What's wrong with it?"

"It's gone," he said.

6

So Kendall Glynn, the poor bastard, had been her father. Interesting, as well as sad, strange and uncomfortable. The latter, both because I distrust coincidences and because I suddenly realized a feeling of guilt over the way Lange had handled things. Funny, he had not. He had felt it the most civilized way of dealing with the situation because he abhorred violence, whereas I would simply have waited for the proper moment and shot the fellow myself. Not that I would not have felt guilty about that, but it would have been a different kind of guilt—a bit cleaner, to my way of thinking.

I thought about him as I worked the lock on the door to the Supplies vault. Jenkins and Winkel were far up the hall, in Storage, wrestling Lange's body onto ice. It seemed a good thing, not just to give them something to do until Gene arrived and I could address them all together as an alternative to meshing, but to have them actually touch the dead reality as well. It might make it a little easier for them to accept what had to be done.

It had been around sixteen years ago, so Glenda was too young to remember it well. Though of course she knew about it—too much and not enough. I/we/it/the nexus had occupied Lange's now cold form in those days, and Kendall Glynn had had to be stopped. He had been sufficiently vocal concerning his ideas to keep me both aware and wary for several years. In a lesser man, I would not have been so concerned. But Glynn was more than a master of engineering. He was one of those scientist-artists who comes along every few centuries to justify the existence of that overworked word "genius." His colleagues respected, envied, admired him; his name was known to the man on the belt as well as the man in the lab. Though it was not until his late forties that he married and fathered Glenda, there was nothing especially

108

misanthropic about him, as is often the case with brilliant men who spend their first thirty or so years being misunderstood. He was engaging, rather than belligerent, for a man who was out to destroy most of the orderly traditions of society and fill the cart with a new species of apple. He was the last real revolutionary I had known, and I respected him. As Lange, though, my main feeling was one of apprehension.

When I learned that things had gotten beyond the talking stage, that he was actually preparing a presentation for the Council and had apparently obtained sufficient support from several representatives to have his request for a pilot project put to a vote, I paid him a visit in my Jess Borgen persona, an old Fellow of the Academy of Sciences. I remembered that day and that body well, as my prostate was giving me a good deal of trouble and I had had to stop off several times on the way over to his place . . .

Kendall was not the lean, scholarly type. He was somewhat short and stocky, with rather rugged features and a thick mane of black hair only slightly frosted above the ears. His most striking feature was his eyes; they were magnified enormously by corrective lenses, especially the left one, and gave the impression that they had looked upon just about everything, could see through just about anything. Considering my own situation, I found this somewhat disconcerting. In fact, it was not for completely urological reasons that after only a few minutes' conversation I had to excuse myself from his welter of globes, star charts, work tables, drawing boards, eco-injection module-mockups and his computer-access station. It was because I had realized that here was a man who just might be able to pull it off, the thing that others had only mumbled about occasionally over the years.

"But the eighteen worlds of the House are already grossly terratype," he had said, "or we would not have located the Wings on them," in response to my, "But each one represents a radically unique environment."

"And you want to thrust people out into them before they are ready?"

"The people or the worlds?" and he had smiled.

"Both."

"Yes," he said. "They can reside in the modules while conducting the planoforming."

"Granting for a moment that it would be to our advantage to adapt the exo-environments, why bother with the intermediary stage? Why not do the work from the House itself, and when things are ready those who want can move out and take advantage of it?"

"No," he said. "I'm afraid," and his voice was very soft and he was no longer looking at me, but at the array of globes on the table to his right. "I consider the House an evolutionary dead end for the human race," he went on. "We have created a static, unyielding environment, to which man must either adapt or go under. Being the durable, adaptable creature that he is, he has not gone under. In the span of only a few centuries, he has changed considerably."

"Yes, he has worn off a lot of rough edges, has become a more rational, more controlled being."

"I do not like that last adjective at all."

"I meant self-controlled."

He made a noise halfway between a chuckle and a couple of snorts, and I excused myself to visit his washroom.

We talked for close to two hours, but that was the real point of contention right there. I did not question the physical feasibility of his proposals. I was certain that all of the worlds in question could indeed be made habitable for man. I was also reasonably satisfied that the various life-support systems he had worked out for those planets which would require them would adequately serve to shelter their inhabitants while the terraforming was going on. I also had no doubt that his other pet project, a new program of interstellar exploration in faster-than-light vehicles, would result in the discovery of new worlds, some of which might be eminently suitable for human use. Whether these were to be pursued simultaneously, as he desired, or only in part, any part, was immaterial to me.

My real concern was over the threat it represented to the House. I was not afraid of what was Out There, but rather of what the availability of Out There would do to what was In Here. It was obvious that his programs were on a collision course with my own.

"What is it that you have against the House?" I asked him, half-joking, at one point.

"It has already succeeded in conditioning much of what is left of the human race," he said, "to behave at the reaction level of a herd of cows. Someday a bull is going to come along and that is the position in which he is going to find us."

"I have to take issue with that," I said. "The House is the first place in the history of the human race where people have succeeded in living together peacefully. They are finally learning to cooperate rather than compete. I see this as a strength, not a weakness."

His eyes narrowed within their pools, staring at me as if seeing me for the first time. Then, "No," he said. "They are beaten over the head if they do not cooperate. Their brains are scrambled, they are shot full of drugs and subjected to therapy to adjust them to an unnatural norm if they are not peaceable in terms of that norm. They become well-programmed claustrophiles. But in learning to live together in the House and love it, I fear that we are sacrificing our ability to live anywhere else. The House cannot endure forever. Its end may also be the end of the human race."

"Ridiculous!" I said. I might have argued over the durability of the House. I might have argued that the dispersion of the race over eighteen separate worlds was a pretty strong factor in favor of its continuance. But both of these arguments would have been specious. My real disagreement with him lay in the interpretation of what the House was doing to people. I could not argue this point fully, however, without explaining my part in matters and giving him an idea as to my overall plan. So I settled back into my Establishment role and said, "Ridiculous!"

With a small smile that was mostly upper lip and malicious, he turned my comment and nodded.

"Yes, I suppose so," he said. "It is ridiculous that the situation managed to reach the point that it did. It would be a little more encouraging in terms of racial sanity if there were some valid devil theory of history, if some person or group could be singled out as sponsor of this madness." He sighed. "However, I am hoping that we can learn from our mistakes, in time."

111

I felt uncomfortable at this, and was able to switch the conversation over to the details of several of his accommodation systems. They were all of them, unfortunately, very well designed. I was determined that they, at least, would not be wasted, eventually.

If only I could have spotted some technical flaws in his work or some major defect in his concepts . . . But no. He had been too thorough. He was just too good. If only he had, I could have had him discredited on those grounds, could have stopped the project that way. If only . . .

There was enough interest in his work to worry me. I was already whipping up an opposition among the conservatives on the Council and in the Academy, but I was not at all that certain that I could see the thing soundly defeated—and it would require a good trouncing to keep it from rising again to plague me.

So, my Lange-incarnation reasoned, there is an alternative to attacking a man's ideas.

A comprehensive check by the Bandit failed to turn up anything juicy and exploitable on the man. Dull or discreet, it did not matter. I could not find my weapon in his past.

I winced as I reviewed my latter ego's thinking, his decision, his action upon it. I had certainly changed a lot in a few generations.

During the next week, we removed five girls from the neighborhood, ranging in age from about five to around seven, at unobtrusive and coverable times during their daily schedules. They were subjected to hypnotics and viewed movies of Kendall while they received suggestions as to what he had said and done during the past few months. It was decided that two of the girls should actually have been molested, and the hymen was surgically broken by Serafis and minor vaginal infections instigated. One would come forth with the revelation, the accusation, the other would duplicate it, the remaining three would provide stories about the dirty old man with the pocket full of candy bars. The girls would of course be treated later by proper medical authorities and made to forget what they believed to have actually occurred. Thus did we salve our collective conscience over the girls.

It happened exactly as we had desired. Once the news got out, Kendall was ruined, the project was ruined and, by association, stars became an even dirtier word. Once he was sent up for his brainwash, it was definitely all over.

I recalled his abhorrence of adjustive techniques, but it never occurred to us that he might be a genuine violence-prone patho, by Lange's definitions, a real throwback. I guess we should have recalled his reply to our casual question, as we headed toward the washroom for the last time, "What will you do if you lose out, badly?" He had stared down at his slippers, bunched and unbunched his toes a couple times within them, then said, "It's all over for us if it doesn't pass." That's all.

About four weeks later, he hanged himself in his quarters in the Dispensary. Glenda must have been about five or six at the time.

While we deplored violence, we did not feel especially guilty about it. We tended to look upon what had occurred as one of those unfortunate, unforeseen things that sometimes happen when you are just doing your job. Also, it was then impossible for us to entertain the possibility of any sort of connection between Kendall and Mr. Black. Black had been deemed dead in my day, and memories of the man were duly erased when Old Lange sacrificed me. Now that I was back, however, the entire Kendall Glynn incident took on a different, more sinister appearance. Unlike my successors, though, I felt rotten about the way things had been handled. I realized that a debt of honor existed toward Glenda.

I thought about this as the clock ticked its way toward opening and Lange's remains were stashed in the cooler. This, and a lot of other things. Of course, I was going to go after Glenda. She knew something—possibly quite important—that she wanted to tell me. Even if she did not, however, I would have gone because she had asked me to, and because of the very strong possibility that she was in danger.

When the vault finally opened, I entered and removed a variety of things I might be needing. I hauled them all off to the little lounge, leaving this vault open behind me, also.

"Library! Cubicle 18237!" Glenda had kept repeating. Since she had not added a Wing designation, this indicated that she meant Library, Cubicle 18237 of the Wing we then occupied.

... Wing 5, of which the Bandit had verified Jenkins' bit of news. As of but a brief while ago, the subways had stopped running and all communications had terminated. It was as if Wing 5 had suddenly ceased to exist.

After I had deposited my gear, I returned to Comp, where I ran another check with the Bandit. It reconfirmed the initial report I had received, with no new developments. A survey of my private subway system to Wing 5 showed all lines to be operational, however. This was as I had expected. Their power source for my uses was located here, not there. Even if it had not been, I had a funny feeling that they might still be working. There seemed to be a pattern emerging, and I had a part in it.

It was not very long before Winkel and Jenkins reentered.

"All set?" I asked.

"Yes," Winkel replied. "Listen, we have a right to know what's going on—"

"Of course," I said. "You will."

"When?"

"We will wait awhile longer to see whether Gene is coming."

"Why not just mesh with him and find out?"

"I'll be talking about that, too."

I turned and walked toward the door.

"What should we do now?" Jenkins asked me.

"I think it would be a good idea for you to wait here for Gene, to turn off the klaxon when he arrives."

"Why not just turn it off now?"

I returned to the control panel and switched our defense system from manual back to automatic. I also removed the pistol from my pocket and set it on the countertop.

"Because it just may be that someone else will come through," I said, turning on the screen and the speaker.

"Who?" said Jenkins.

"I'll tell you about that later, too."

"What should we do if it is someone else?"

"If the equipment doesn't get him, you'd better."

"Even if it means using that gun?"

"Even if it means using your teeth and fingernails. I'm going up to the lounge now. I have some things to do."

I could hear them talking as I headed on up the hall,

but I could not make out what they were saying. Just as well, I suppose.

I entered the lounge, crossed it and activated the window. The temperature had dropped slightly and the moon had traveled a considerable distance, shifting the shadow patterns about. The light from the ruin was no longer visible. I stared for perhaps a minute, still puzzling over its earlier occurrence, then turned my attention to the equipment I had fetched.

Stripping to my undergarments, I donned lightweight body armor that protected me from groin to neckline. I put on full-length black trousers then, because I wanted to wear some explosives taped along the inside of my left calf. A heavy-caliber revolver went into a belt holster to be covered by a white, short-sleeved shirt. Something from outside disturbed me as I was taping the stiletto to my left forearm. A movement?

I lit a cigarette and spent a few minutes staring out the window.

The flicker. Yes. It came again. Once, twice . . .

My observations were interrupted by the sound of the klaxon. I departed the lounge immediately and headed down the hall. The alarm ceased before I had gone twenty feet, so I slowed to a walk. I continued on far enough to see that it was Gene, our youngest member, then waved to him and turned back.

"Wait!" I heard him call out, followed by the sounds of rapid footfalls.

"I'll be with you in a few minutes," I called back. "Go on into the Comp room. Jenkins and Winkel are there."

The running continued and I decided the hell with him. I had already told him where I was going, and I was not about to stand there and justify myself.

He caught up with me just as I was about to reenter the lounge. Whatever he was about to say was forgotten, however, as we made the turn together and the burst of light hit us. He gripped my arm and we stood there for a moment, unmoving.

Then I stepped into the room and he released his hold and followed me across it. We moved to the window and stood there squinting into the light. Yes, it was coming from the ruin all right.

From behind us, I heard Winkel make a brief noise, like, "Wha—?"

Then the light was gone, and everything out there was as it had been before.

I reached out and opaqued the thing again. I moved toward the nearer chair, where I had been standing earlier, and arrived there just as Jenkins burst into the room.

"What is going on?" he inquired, searching our faces.

"Nothing," I said, picking up a light-gray jacket and pulling it on, "now."

I dropped a handful of extra ammo and two gas grenades into my left side pocket. Three small fragmentation bombs went into my right.

"We are going back to Comp, right now," I announced. "Someone must be on duty there at all times, until this thing is over. There must be no unauthorized visitors."

"Have there ever been?" Jenkins asked.

"Yes."

"Who?"

"I'll tell you about it in Comp. Come on."

They followed me into the hall. As we headed down it, Gene said, "What was that light?"

"I don't know."

"It could be something important."

"I am certain that it is."

We entered Comp and I moved to adjust the subway equipment to take me to Wing 5. Before I could set the circuits, however, Winkel stepped in front of me and stood there, hands on his hips.

"All right," he said. "What's the story? Why didn't you mesh?"

"Because," I said, "you would have been radically changed by the process, and I want you just the way you are until I have decided what I am going to do about my condition."

"What condition? What is the matter?"

I sighed, lit a cigarette, moved to his right and seated myself on the countertop, facing the three of them.

"I pulled pins seven and six," I said.

"You *what*?"

"You heard me."

116

There was silence. I had expected a blizzard of questions, but they just stared.

"It had to be done," I said. "We were being killed left and right, and there was no apparent reason, no way of stopping it. By unlocking generations of experience, I hoped to find something—information, a weapon. I was scared, too."

Winkel dropped his eyes and nodded.

"I would have done the same thing," he said.

"So would I," said Gene.

"I guess I would have, too," Jenkins said, joining in the effort to make me feel better. "Did you find something?"

"Yes, I believe I did. But it is rather complicated, and I only have time to hit some of the highlights now."

"Before you do," Winkel said, "tell us one thing: Who are you now, really?"

"I am the same person I was before," I said, feeling that I was lying and feeling, too, their need for reassurance that everything was not coming apart at the same moment. "The only difference is that now I have access to all the memories of old Lange and Winton, as well as those of Jordan which Winton did not choose to sacrifice."

But he saw, I think, and persisted.

"Of them all, who do you most feel like?" he said.

"Myself! Damn it!" I said. I was half-minded to mesh then and there and remove all cause for argument and explanation both. But I held to my conviction that this might not be wise in terms of whatever personal editing I might eventually be required to undertake. Also, from the look on his face, I believed that Winkel might be prepared to resist the mesh at this time. So, "There was some influence, of course," I said. "That was unavoidable. Fortunately, it is of benefit in the present situation. I am still basically me, though."

He still looked unconvinced, but further insistence was not going to strengthen my statement—just the opposite, perhaps—so I decided to let it rest at that and get down to essentials.

"It appears that, several generations ago, an individual became aware of our existence," I began. "How he learned of us remains a mystery. But he demonstrated his knowledge of the personal identities of all the members of the family at that time. He did this in a manner that bore

117

a close resemblance to our present plight. He attempted to murder all of us. He was obviously unsuccessful, possibly because the tendency was still strong within us to strike back instantly. We did not, however, succeed in obtaining his destruction, rehabilitation or even—for that matter— knowledge of his identity. He did succeed in killing three of us before we increased our wariness and the variety of our defenses to the point where several further attempts on his part were frustrated and he became the hunted. We came close to capturing him on two occasions, but he managed to escape us both times. Then he vanished. The attacks ceased. Years passed. Nothing.

"While we did not forget what had occurred," I went on, "the absence of the peril allowed for a gradual return of some feelings of security. Perhaps he was dead, we felt. Or had given up on his vendetta for reasons as inscrutable as those which had caused him to embark upon it. Whatever his disposition, he apparently took his knowl- edge of our affairs with him, for there was never any indication, anywhere else, of an awareness of our exis- tence.

"Then, almost nine years later, he struck again, as suddenly as before. His planning and his coordination were very good. He got five of us at that time. He might have done even better, had not Benton been able to shoot him before he died himself. He was apparently pretty badly wounded, but he managed to get away before we reached the scene. Then, again, nothing. For several years. We assumed he had died as a result of his wounds."

"How do you know it was the same man?" Gene asked me.

"An assumption," I replied, "based primarily upon the similar pattern of attack. We also have a gross physical description, from the terminal impressions of several of his victims. And we have other data, such as his blood type—"

"Was it the same man who shot you?" Winkel asked.

"In light of what I know now, yes. I believe that it was."

"Where there any other attacks besides the two you have described?"

"Yes. Many years after the passing of Jordan, during the time when Winton was nexus, he came here, to Wing

118

Null. The nature of his intentions was never clear to us. We have no idea what he would have done had the place been unoccupied, as it is so much of the time. As it was, Winton just happened to be here—here in Comp, as a matter of fact—when he arrived. The klaxon sounded and Winton picked him up on the screen. Interestingly, he had succeeded in avoiding the automatic defenses. How he achieved this remains a mystery. Winton headed for the hall and startled him there, opening fire immediately. He fled, returning the fire, and although he was wounded he succeeded in throwing himself across the grid and making an exit. Winton returned here and traced him, discovering he had gone to the Chapel on Wing 7. He immediately meshed with the others, and we attempted an intercept there. But beyond a few gory traces, he was not to be found."

"That was the last such occurrence—until recently, that is?"

"Yes. Old Lange retained the memory as a precaution. Lange erased it as a useless violence-reminder when he became nexus, though. So much time had passed that it seemed a safe assumption that our enemy was dead."

"A mistake."

"Obviously."

"He left no clues?"

"A few here and there. Dead ends, all. For instance, he dropped a tool kit when I—Winton shot him. It proved to have been stolen from a maintenance locker in the Cellar of Wing 11. The trail ended there."

"No prints, no traces of any sort on the tools or their container?"

"None. He always wore gloves at the proper time. Careful sort. We spent a long while checking on everybody even remotely associated with the maintenance locker. Again, nothing. But the nature of the tools themselves gave rise to some interesting speculations."

"Of what sort?"

"The tools were of the type a person might choose to work on the locks we had on the vaults then. Does that remind you of anything?"

"The missing clone!"

"Exactly. Our big, unsolved mystery, over a century old

119

now. One day a clone is gone from its locker, never to be seen again. Where? How? Why? No answers. Absolutely useless to anyone but the family. Supposedly inaccessible to anyone but us. Gone. That was why we installed fancier locks on the vaults and built the defense system. We changed our subway setup, too. Despite these precautions, though, someone reached us again and it was only by chance that we were able to stop him. The connection seems unavoidable, though the motive is anybody's guess. We revamped the whole security framework, achieving what we have today. As the years went by, we relaxed again. Eventually, so much time passed that we felt safe in allowing ourselves to forget, piece by piece, everything but the nagging fact of the missing clone, which for some reason no one felt quite up to erasing. I feel our Mr. Black is involved with the whole thing.

"Therefore," I concluded, "I want a man on this panel at all times, monitoring the arrival station. If we should receive an unwelcome visitor and he is able to avoid the automatic defenses, you must be ready to switch over to manual immediately. Also, I want you to break out something heavier than trank guns and carry them until this thing is settled."

Their faces were blank, puzzled, irritated, going from left to right.

"What exactly are we supposed to do with Mr. Black?" Winkel said.

"Well, I would like to have the contents of his head intact," I told him. "But if they happen to get in the way of a bullet, that's all right, too."

I moved to a panel and set my course for Wing 5.

"You haven't told us everything yet, have you?" he asked.

"Just essentials. Time is important. You are next in line for the nexus, though. If anything happens to me, you will wind up knowing more than I do now. That is one of the advantages of serial immortality."

"I may not want to have it all."

". . . and you need not keep it. That is one of the advantages of partial suicide."

I turned away and headed toward the door.

"Do you intend to bring him here for interrogation?"

I paused and shook my head.

"My goal is a more modest one," I said, "I just want to kill the son of a bitch."

A minute later I was in a dark, silent place on Wing 5.

7

I emerged cautiously, but no one seemed to be about. Fine. I closed the black door behind me and moved away quickly.

Something was wrong, and it took me several seconds to sort out my impressions.

It was the stillness. It was eerie, hearing nothing beyond the echoes of my own footsteps. There were no machine sounds, no humming, whirring background noises; even the beltways had been muted. The air seemed much warmer than usual and hung motionless about me. The dimness was much heavier than normal, though I could see an area of illumination, faint, far off to my right.

I suppressed my curiosity as to the light source and continued on in the direction I had chosen. That way lay the nearest jackpole, a jet tower rooted in a wilderness of broken outlines and vanishing into infinity. I would have to walk its spiral, I feared.

Was Mr. Black waiting for me somewhere between here and there, I wondered? Possibly, knowing our use of the black doors, knowing that I would come to Wing 5.

Was this a mad extreme to which he had gone in his effort to destroy us, or was it the other way around? Was this some part of a thing long in the planning, to which our removal was but an ancillary provision?

Either way, it mattered little now. I was as ready as possible, under the circumstances.

I walked on through the blackout. Had there been a breakdown in the cellar, or was the power being diverted elsewhere to meet some emergency?

And what of Glenda? What did she know? What was her part in this thing?

Then I froze in my tracks and had my hand on my gun, half-drawing it from the holster. What—?

A chord. Then another. Then angry, throbbing music. Violent. Jerkily played. It was an organ, suddenly come to life in a recess not too far to my left. Moments later, I recognized the music, strange sounds for a place of worship and meditation: the *Damnation of Faust*.

I followed it, of course. There are circumstances under which the anomalous should be courted. Ignorance is one of them.

As I moved diagonally toward the entrance to the area, I caught a glimpse of a weird tableau within. A somewhat disheveled man in clerical garb was seated at the keyboard. A small candelabra gave him light from atop the instrument, and two wine bottles kept it company.

I advanced, entered. He smiled at me, closed his eyes and continued playing. As I moved nearer, he opened them again and his smile vanished, to be replaced by a loose-jawed look of horror. His fingers stumbled into a final discord and he slumped forward, shaking.

I stood there for a few moments, undecided as to what I should do. He resolved the matter, however, by raising his head and lowering his hands from his face. He stared at me, panting, then said, "Don't keep me in suspense. What is the verdict?"

"What do you mean?" I said.

"Has my petition been granted?" he asked, his eyes dropping to regard my feet, then turning toward the altar.

I followed his glance and saw that the altar was in disarray, with the crucifix inverted above it.

I gave a small shrug. So the local preacher had decided to switch sides. Was it worth the time it would take to find out what had prompted it?

Possibly, I decided, since something recent and traumatic was doubtless involved.

"Well?" he said.

"Who do you think I am?" I asked.

He smiled slyly and bowed his head.

"I saw where you came from," he said. "I have been watching the black door since I made my offering. When I saw you emerge, I played propitious music."

"I see. And what do you seek to gain by this?"

"You have heard me, you have come. You know what I would have."

123

"Do not try my patience!" I said. "I want to hear you say it! Now!"

His eyes widened and he threw himself prostrate before me.

"I meant no offense!" he said. "I seek only to please you!"

"What prompts this sudden appreciation of that which is most fitting and proper?"

"When it happened, and people began to come to me, with stories, of the terror . . . I held services. People kept coming. Finally, I was granted a glimpse. Before the power failed. Before the evacuation order. I saw that we had been forsaken. I knew then that we had been given over to destruction, and I thought, 'Make to yourselves friends of the mammon of unrighteousness; that, when ye fail, they may receive you into everlasting habitations.'"

"Why do you feel you have been forsaken?"

"For our presumption, our resentments, our secret desires—"

"I mean, what happened?"

He raised his head, looked up at me.

"You mean the explosions and all?"

"Yes. And get up off the floor."

He scrambled to his feet and backed away. When he came up against the bench, I nodded and said, "Sit down."

He did, and, "The explosions, just a few hours ago," he said, "when they tore through the wall, they showed us—the stars . . . Oh God!" He looked comically startled, then added, "I'm sorry."

"Which level?"

"Living Room," he said, glancing at his bottle atop the organ.

I sighed. Good. That was down four, whereas the Library was only two levels below me. All the way through the wall . . . It must have been quite an explosive, that.

"What happened after the explosions?" I said.

"There was a rush to get away," he said. "Then when everybody realized what had happened, there was a rush to go and look out." He licked his lips, looked at the bottle again. "Then another rush to get away," he finished.

"Go ahead and drink some," I said.

He seized the bottle, put it to his lips and threw his

124

head back. I watched his Adam's apple do pushups off his collar.

Wing 5. At least, he had picked a fairly congenial planet for his catastrophe—the atmosphere was breathable, though somewhat irritating, and the temperature was bearable at night.

"And you went and looked?" I asked.

He lowered the bottle, nodded and began to cough. Then, after a few moments, he pointed at the altar.

"I saw eternity," he said. "The sky just goes on and on forever. And I saw the lights in the heavens. I smelled the fumes of the Pit. People were screaming and fainting. Others were pushing forward. Some were running. Some went out into it, I think, and were lost. They herded us back finally, and off that level. They may have sealed it off by now. Many people came to the Chapel. There were services going on all over. I held three myself. I felt stranger and stranger all the while. I knew that it was Judgment Day. I knew that we were all unworthy. It is the end. The House is falling and the heavens have been opened. Man is insignificant, worthless. I knew that when I looked on eternity." He paused to take another drink, then continued, "After my last service, I knew that I could not go on. I could not go on praying for deliverance from that which I knew we deserved. Better to embrace it, I decided. So I came to this section which was not in use. All of the others are over that way." He gestured in the direction of the illumination—candles, doubtless. "Here I did what I thought most fitting," he concluded. "Take me, master," and he hiccuped.

"I am not he whom you have summoned," I said, and I turned to go.

"No!" I heard him cry; and I heard the bottle fall, and I heard him curse and scramble after it. Then, "I saw where you came from!" he shrieked. "You came through the black door!"

"You are mistaken," I said.

"No! I know what I saw! Who are you?"

His plight must have moved me a little further up the philosophical alley than I had realized, for I actually considered his question for a moment and answered it honestly.

"I don't really know," I said, and I kept moving.

"Liar!" he called out. "Father of Lies!"

Then he began to weep.

"So *this* is Hell . . ." I heard him saying as I departed.

I moved away quickly, thinking about the reactions of others. I wondered whether he could be typical. I thought not. I hoped not. He was an aberrant, that was all. His was not the direction in which we had been steering them.

I walked at a brisk clip, paralleling the still beltway that led off toward the jackpole. Small knots of figures moved along it, passing in both directions through the gloom. What light there was came from those appliances and signs equipped with their own power units, from candlelit sections of the Chapel, luminous trouble-plates and hand-beams borne by the pedestrians. And during the next five or ten minutes, I passed two slow processions where everyone bore a lighted candle. I saw no one who was not part of some group.

I thought again of the power loss. This sort of emergency would hardly call for an action that would require most of the electrical output, even for one level. No. There had to have been a bit of simultaneous mischief in the Cellar. Which indicated a time bomb rather than teamwork, as Black had always impressed me as playing a completely solitary hand. The timing, of everything, was very important. The attack on the family, the hole in the wall, the loss of power. I could feel the pattern there, although I could not understand it. It was quite possible that I never would. I would probably have to kill him before he could tell me. And the alternative made no provision for our enlightenment either. Pity. All that planning, timing, coordination—with success entailing the destruction of the only ones capable of appreciating your work. Kind of sad, any way you looked at it, whatever happened.

Before too long, I reached the jackpole and entered there. It was dark and still. I began walking down its spiral. I hurried past the next level—the Bedroom—for I could see clearly there because of several fires, one near at hand. People were rushing about in their vicinities, and at first I thought that they had either panicked or become irrational and started the things themselves. But no. Most of them seemed to be beating at them or soaking them. Something appeared to be wrong with the sprinkler sys-

126

tem. There were fire vehicles all about and more on the way—both in the air and on the ground. Groups of cranes hung frozen above them in a variety of attitudes.

As I reached the next level, my destination, I was pleased not to observe any disasters in progress. There were numerous small lights in motion below me. Personal handbeams, it seemed. I was glad that Mr. Black had not seen fit to indulge in incendiarism in the Library, too.

Quite a few people seemed to be entering at the base of the jackpole, but so far I had encountered no one. Which indicated that they were all heading downward. In the direction of the damaged Living Room. I wondered at their purpose.

Going over my mental map, I recalled an emergency-vehicle hatch about a quarter-mile in the direction of the far wall. I resolved to appropriate whatever might be available for flight, as the number Glenda had given me was a good distance away.

When I reached floor level, I stood aside as people hurried in past me and headed for the downward winding. They spoke excitedly, some near-hysterically, and many of them carried parcels.

"Where are you going?" I asked a man who had come running, and then paused to catch his breath.

"Out," he said.

I could not believe that he meant what he seemed to mean.

"You mean outside?" I said. "Out of the House?"

"Where else? It's coming apart around us, the House."

"But you can't—I mean, it's sealed off, it's quarantined down there, isn't it?"

He laughed.

"Take my advice and come along," he said. "You wouldn't believe what it is like out there."

"What is it like?"

"It's beautiful!"

"But—"

He hurried away then and was quickly out of sight.

I was of course disturbed. Overheard snatches of conversation indicated a variety of motives for this small-scale exodus, ranging from a fear of the imminent collapse of the House to a desire for adventure, a morbid fascination with the effects of disaster, religious fervor, scientific interest

127

and just plain primate curiosity. Whatever the reasons, the results of the action would be around for a long while. I did not relish the introduction of unpredictables into my closed, controlled system.

There was nothing to be done about it just then, however. I pushed my way out the door and hurried in the direction of the vehicles bay.

I sprinted the final hundred yards or so to the bay, the doors of which stood open. I shone the beam I had appropriated from the man who had bumped against me and begun cursing me on the way out. There appeared to be two vehicles down to my left. I climbed over the edge, hung for a moment at arms' length and dropped to the landing stage.

One of the fliers was blocked up for maintenance work and the other was secured in a parking area. I checked the fuel level of the second one, unchocked its wheels and with considerable effort managed to roll it out onto the stage.

It started quickly, and within three minutes I was airborne. I moved carefully, fairly near to the ceiling, my forward and side lights switched to their brightest, avoiding cranes and pillars as I went. Below, it was like a photographic negative of moths about a flame, all those little lights flitting toward the black tower.

Cubicle 18237. That was quite a distance across the room. Periodically, I dropped lower, to shine my light on coordinate markers. Another flier passed me, going in the opposite direction, but I received no signals from it.

I withdrew my mind from thoughts of people's reactions and turned my attention to my own affairs. My enemy had planned things carefully, and I doubted he was about to slack off at this point. I thought of Glenda once again, and of the possibility that I was heading for some sort of trap. She had helped me earlier—a good sign—and she was Kendall's daughter—which was sufficient, to my way of thinking, to justify any action she cared to take against me, were she aware of my part in things. What moved her, and what were her intentions? Was Black using her? If so, how? Though I pushed my mind through a series of mazes, I could come up with no approach other than the direct. There were simply too many variables. Any attempt to be especially devious could boomerang on me.

Most of the effects of Black's trank would have worn off by now, I knew.

When I came into her section, I located an open space near to considerable cover in the form of tables, partitions and machines, landed the flier, killed its lights and engine, and disembarked. It was quite dark, but I had swept the area with my spotlight before coming down. It had seemed to be empty of people.

I rushed for cover, nevertheless, and began a circuitous route that would take me into the area of the cubicle I sought.

I spent several minutes working my way toward the door of 18237 and investigating the vicinity. There were no ambushers that I could detect. But while the glow of candlelight emerged from the windows of the adjacent quarters, Glenda's were dark.

I approached with the pistol in my hand, rapped upon her door with its barrel, waited.

As I stood there, I wondered whether she had been caught up in the general confusion, or whether any of a number of other things had worked to keep her from returning. If she were not present, I resolved to enter and wait for her.

As I moved to knock again, however, I heard a noise from within and the door was unlatched and opened partway. Glenda stood there in the faint light, and her eyes moved from my face to the gun and back again quickly.

"Yes?" she said. "What do you want?"

"We parted rather abruptly a little while ago," I said. "But you invited me to drop by."

Her features constricted and relaxed in the space of an instant. Her voice was normal, even cheerful, as she then said, "Of course! Come in! Come in!" But she raised her right hand as if to bar my way as she said it. Then as I hesitated, puzzled, she hurled herself against me.

As I stumbled back to retain my footing and she slipped to the floor, I heard the sound of a shot from within. She had succeeded in thrusting me far enough to the side to be out of the line of fire, however. I immediately put two rounds through the door, just to let him know I was not standing there doing nothing, waiting to be shot at again, the while shouting to Glenda to get the hell out of sight.

129

She did not really need the encouragement, though, as she vanished quickly and soundlessly in the direction from which I had come.

I threw myself sprawling and slid up against the wall, as I had been in line of sight from both windows and had no idea where he was inside. My foresight was repaid as the nearest window was shattered by another shot. I fetched out one of my two gas grenades, activated it and lobbed it through the window. Moments later, I followed it with the second one.

Hugging the wall, I crawled backward, the better to cover the near windows as well as the door and the window on its far side.

I waited. I heard the things go off, with soft popping sounds, and after a time ghostly tendrils drifted out through the shattered window and the still-gaping door.

While I was wondering what was going to happen next, it happened.

There came an explosion and fragments of the wall fell all over me. I was engulfed in a cloud of dust and gas. I fought to keep from coughing, my eyes watered and I could see nothing but a blurred haze. I felt as if I had been kicked in several dozen places along my back and side. I jerked my pistol free of the mess and kept blinking my eyes to clear them.

I barely caught sight of the figure leaping through the rubble, right on the heels of the explosion. It was somewhere in the vicinity just vacated by the door. He passed to the right, running, and I fired after him. I missed, of course, and he kept going.

Shaking off debris, I struggled to my feet and plunged after him, staggering through my first several steps. He was still in sight, and I had no intention of losing him this time.

Coming to a partition, he whirled suddenly and fired back at me before passing behind it, not waiting to see the effect of his shot. I felt a stinging sensation along my left forearm, and I raised my weapon and put three rounds through the partition. I veered to reach an alcove then, and reloaded quickly once I had achieved it.

I dropped to all fours before I looked around the corner, and I pulled back quickly when I saw him, leaning around the edge of his partition and pointing a weapon in my direction. The shot followed a moment later, fairly high and wide.

I fired back before I withdrew to prime an explosive grenade. When I exposed myself to hurl it, he fired again. I drew back immediately, primed another grenade and sent it after the first.

The first one exploded while the second was still in the air. By the time the second explosion came, my weapon was back in my right hand. I rounded the corner and raced toward what was left of the partition.

There was no one about when I reached the wrecked area. I halted, casting about in all directions, and then I caught sight of a fleeing shadow, far off to the left. I plunged after him.

He was crossing an open area, heading toward a warren of narrow aisles and reading booths. I ran as fast as I could, and the distance between us narrowed. I fired a shot and he jerked, stumbled, recovered and kept going.

When he reached a post at the edge of the area, he threw himself against it, turned suddenly and began shooting. I was out in the open with nothing to duck behind, so I kept going, raising my own weapon and firing back at him.

The only reason I could see for his missing me under those conditions was the fact that he was injured. He emptied his weapon at me, realized that he did not have time to reload it, turned and lurched off up the nearest aisle. Mine had been emptied also by then, and I refused to allow him the time it would take me to reload. I pursued him up the aisle.

Ahead, he turned left into a side passage or booth, and I slowed. While it was still sufficiently dark to confuse my sense of perspective somewhat, I realized with a start that the overhead lights were glowing faintly now and could easily have been doing so for the past several minutes. A bad sign, the power coming back so quickly, when I wanted to get him and clear out before any measure of order returned to the place.

I jammed my pistol back within my shirt and tore the stiletto loose from where it rode my forearm. It was moist and slightly bent, and it occurred to me that it had been grazed by a bullet and driven to break my skin—the stinging I had felt earlier.

131

I swung wide at the corner where he had turned, dropping into a crouch, blade low.

He sprang at me. He had a blade of some sort—I saw its faint gleam as it came toward me—but he held it awkwardly and his first strike, which I was able to push aside, was faster than anything that followed. He blocked mine with his forearm and slashed at my abdomen. My armor deflected this, and after a few feints I was able to sink my blade up to the hilt in his stomach. He made a bubbling noise, stiffened and sagged against me. I caught him and lowered him to the floor.

I struck a light to better study his face. I tugged at his hair and it came away; it was a dark wig. Beneath, his own hair was white. Yes, it was indeed the same man who had occupied the power chair, who had gotten Lange to order him a drink and then shot him. Mr. Black.

And he stared at me and smiled.

"Jordan . . . ?" he said.

"Winton," I replied.

"Close, close . . . It couldn't have been anyone later. Those creampuffs . . ."

"Why?" I said. "Why did you do it?"

He shook his head.

"You'll find out. Soon," he said. "Oh, very soon!"

"What?"

He grimaced, then forced the smile once more.

"I could have taken you—with the knife—if I had wanted . . ." he said. "Think about it—"

He died then, grinning at me, and suddenly I realized what he had meant.

8

Mesh—No!

He was old, and somewhere along the line he had changed the facial structure a bit more radically than the rest of us, but as I felt his death within my own being and fought to block an abrupt mesh-effect, I realized that Mr. Black was the missing clone.

Gritting my teeth, squeezing my temples, I built walls of resistance about my mind. There is always a meshing when one of us dies, and its effects vary. It does not matter too much, though, since we are all of us contained within one another, "nexus" only being the term by which we refer to the oldest among us, who is automatically head of the family.

Black was indeed one of us, since the terminal mesh-effect was occurring. For all of his life he must have been blocking the ordinary meshings each time that they occurred. Still, as a silent party to our telepathic bond, I could understand his uncanny ability when it came to pursuing us, knowing our whereabouts.

Having dwelled apart from us all of his life, he was totally unfamiliar. The effects of his personality on our own could be catastrophic. They would of course vary in each instance. I had a strong feeling that he would tend to dominate, however.

I held him off. The impulse that had been beating against my mind died down, faded, was gone.

For an instant, Winkel, Gene and Jenkins would think it was me that had died.

Then it would be too late.

Which of them would break first? I wondered. And what would he do when he did?

Damn!

I twisted the blade out of his belly and wiped it on his

jacket. Our wayward brother had certainly stacked the deck. I had to get back to Wing Null immediately to try to deal with whatever catastrophe was about to break loose there. And I was taken by the feeling that I might not be able to.

I dropped the blade into an inside pocket and turned away. Glenda was standing about ten feet up the corridor, digging at her cheek with her fingertips.

"He's dead," she said. "Isn't he?"

"I'm afraid not," I said, going to her and taking her hand away from her face.

I did not release her arm, but used it to turn her gently, back in the direction from which we had come.

"Come with me," I said. "There are things we must talk about, later."

She did not resist as I led her away from the smiling figure and back toward the flier. The lights continued to brighten as we went.

It was not until we were airborne and on our way to the jackpole that she spoke again:

"Where are we going?"

"To a place called Wing Null," I said.

"Where is that?"

"It is too complicated to explain just now."

She nodded.

"I understand about your secret place—that you have one, I mean."

"How is it that you do? Mr. Black?"

"Yes," she said. "What did you mean when you said that he was not dead? I saw you—kill him."

"Only a body died. *He* still exists."

"Where?"

"Wing Null, I fear."

"How? The same way as you—do it?"

"Perhaps. What do you know about it?"

"I am sure that you are somehow Mr. Engel, the man I was with earlier, the man I saw die. You transmigrated some way, and you came to the address I gave you then. I have no idea as to the mechanism involved."

"Mr. Black again? That is where you heard of this?"

"Yes."

"What is he to you?"

"He was my guardian, after my father died and my

134

mother had to be sent away, for treatments. He volunteered and the plat council appointed him. He had been a friend of my father."

"What did he do? What was his occupation?"

"He was a teacher. Classics. He used the name Eibon then. Henry Eibon."

"Why?"

"Originally, he had told me it was a game. You see, I had known him as Mr. Black when he used to visit us. He began using the other name when he became my guardian. Later, of course, I realized that it was more than a game, but I kept my mouth shut because I loved him. He was very good to me. —You say there is a chance that I will see him again soon?"

"I am afraid so."

"Suppose you tell me what he is to you?"

"We have been enemies for a long while. He started the vendetta. I have no idea why."

She was silent as we traveled the remaining distance and I located a deserted area not too far from the jackpole and landed the flier in a three-walled reading lounge. As I helped her out, I said, "Do you?"

"What if I were to say 'yes'?"

I seized her by the shoulders and spun her, so that her face was about eight inches from my own.

"Talk!" I said. "Tell me why!"

"Let me go! I didn't say that I knew!"

I tightened my grip, then relaxed it. I slid my hand down her arm and turned her by the elbow.

"Come on," I said. "We have to go up a couple levels."

If she did not want to talk, I did not have the time to shake the answers out of her. I had wanted to reach her for two reasons: to protect her and to obtain the information it seemed she possessed. Now she seemed to be in no need of protection and unwilling to part with information. But now that I was aware of her special relationship with Black, I felt myself automatically begin thinking of her as something of a hostage. I was not pleased with the discovery of this reaction, but I was not about to abandon it either.

"Basically," she said, as we headed toward the jackpole through the growing light, "you want to keep people in the House, don't you?"

135

"Well," I said, "to be basic and general about it, yes. I think it is a good idea."

"Why?"

"It is the best way I know for people to learn to really live together."

"By forcing them?"

"Of course. When the alternatives to proximity have been removed and aggressive energies are rechanneled, people tend to cooperate rather than compete. Some measure of coercion is needed, though, to set up such a state of affairs."

"Then what happens?"

"What do you mean?"

"Have people changed much, from living in the House?"

"I think they have."

"Will they continue to change?"

"I believe so."

"They will be allowed to go outside when they have reached some ideal point of adaptation?"

"Of course."

"Why 'of course'? Why not right now? Why do you want to see them prisoners until they have changed?"

"They are not prisoners. They can come and go as they please."

"In the House!"

"In the House."

"Why not outside, too?"

My head began to hurt and I became acutely aware of all my other aches and pains. I did not feel like answering her.

Do you want me to?

"Why not?" I decided. "Go ahead, Jordan. Say whatever you want."

Give me your mouth, your throat, your breathing. Relax.

I did this, and moments later he began to speak.

"Turn them loose?" he said. "To diversify, accentuate their differences, to stimulate competition, aggression, violence toward one another? They very nearly succeeded in destroying themselves that way once. Given similar circumstances, they might succeed the next time. To prevent this, man himself needs to be changed. He is not yet what

136

he will be, but he is better than he was. When he has learned to live with himself, peacefully, here in the House, then he will be ready to go outside it."

"But will he still be human?" she said.

"Whatever he is will be human, for that will then be the measure of humanity."

"What gives you the right to make all these judgments?"

"Someone must. Anyone who wants can."

"Mr. Black did. And he disagreed with you. To make the House safe for your nonaggressive, nonviolent ideals, you killed him."

"I shall exist only for so long as I am needed to promote tranquillity, then I, too, shall pass."

"Who is to decide when this time has arrived?"

"I am."

She laughed.

"Can we count on it?" she said.

"I see no reason not to. I have done it many times before."

She shook her head, turned to stare at me. She tried to halt, but I still had hold of her arm and I continued to propel her toward the pole.

"I get the feeling we are talking two different languages or something," she said. "One moment you sound rational, and the next you go off on a tangent. Are you one entity, or is your name Legion?"

I tightened my will like a vise, and "Get thee behind me, Jordan," I said within myself.

All right, I'm going, and he was gone.

"I am myself," I said.

"Should I call you Engel?"

"Why not? It is as good as anything. Tell me why Black wants to get people out of the House."

"He felt it was lobotomizing the race, turning people into vegetables—and that if they finally did make it outside, they would be in no condition to survive."

"Our disagreement then is too basic for argument, since it centers on a matter of interpretation. What has he told you about me?"

"He told me there is a multibodied enemy of the people who feels as you say you feel about things."

"Did he tell you how he came to be aware of this state of affairs?"

"No."

"What did he tell you concerning his own—background?"

"Nothing at all."

"You are lying."

She shrugged.

"What are you going to do about it?"

"Nothing, just now."

We entered the jackpole. People kept hurrying past us, all of them heading downward.

"What if I were to scream?" she said. "What if I were to refuse to accompany you any farther?"

"You will not. You will come without causing any difficulties."

"What makes you think so?"

"I have totally engaged your curiosity, and yours is one of the most active minds in the House."

"What do you know about my mind?"

"I know just about everything there is to know about you."

"Now you are lying."

This time I shrugged, and smiled. We made our way around and upward, upward and around.

". . . You would have tranked me," she said after a time, "and acted as if I had been taken ill."

"Perhaps."

Moments later, I collapsed against the wall, an involuntary cry escaping my lips. She caught my left arm as it flailed the air, and helped to support me as I was taken by spasm after spasm, the world advancing, receding, coming apart, being reassembled about me and within me.

"What is it?" she said.

But I could only gasp, "Wait. Wait . . ."

Finally, things fell together, the center held. I regained my balance, sucked a couple of deep draughts of stale air and began to move once again. Glenda kept hold of my arm and repeated her question several times.

"Good old Mr. Black just murdered two more people," I said, hurrying. "He thinks he has the upper hand now, and if it is any consolation to you, he may be right."

She did not respond, but hurried along with me. A few people rushed past us, heading downward. They ignored us completely. I wondered what had become of the little boy

138

who liked to run in the wrong direction. In my mind's eye, I saw him standing before an enormous hole in the wall, turning to stick out his tongue, then racing on through and out across a starlit field.

When we reached the level of the Chapel things were brighter than they had been, though still not much better than twilight. The soft glow of candlelight came from several new directions. The belts remained dead. I aimed us in the direction from which I had come, wondering if the apostate preacher had passed out yet.

It was Gene and Jenkins who had died, Winkel who had yielded to Black's personality assault. A moment's work with the handiest weapon and he held Wing Null. What now?

Me, of course.

I was the last one left. Once I was out of the way, he could get on with his plans, whatever they might be. I regretted that, if he won, I would probably never understand the exact nature of our relationship, would never know what it was that he had had in mind all along. Finding out would almost be worth the ultimate risk. . . . I shelved that thought for the time being, however.

I wanted to run. I wanted to reach the black door as soon as possible, plunge through it and get things settled, finally. But I was hurting enough as it was and I knew that my reactions had been slowed. There was no sense in arriving all out of breath, too.

I also wanted to say things to Glenda. I wanted to say, "All right, what was it you wanted to tell me when you invited me to your place as I lay dying?" I wanted to tell her that I knew her story about having lost a pack of jobs was a lie, that I knew she held a professorship in engineering. I wanted to ask her why, since she had set me up for an ambush, she had pushed me out of the line of fire at the last moment. I wanted to ask her why she was being so cooperative in accompanying me now. And I was curious whether she was carrying a weapon.

But of course I said none of these things.

We hurried along, passing a few people, ignoring them and being ignored. All of them seemed headed for one or another of the services. In due course, we neared the area of my arrival. There was, unfortunately, a service in progress too near for me to utilize the facility I desired. It

139

took me close to ten minutes to locate another one in a deserted area. I sprang the door and swung it open, climbed up, turned, held out my hand and helped Glenda inside. She did not balk or question this, but followed me down the incline, her hand on my shoulder.

At the rear, I opened the box and fiddled with it, knowing she was watching everything that I did. Well, I could fiddle with her memories, too, later, if there was a later.

The door closed above and behind us. I snapped the box shut and I took up a position in front of Glenda, a primed grenade in my left hand, the pistol in my right. If the defense system was set on automatic, it would not fire when it scanned me, though. If he had it on manual, I was hoping that Glenda's presence would make him hesitate to push buttons. If he did not, we still had my body armor between us and a host of deadlies. Maybe I could knock them out in time.

"I take it this is not a standard procedure," I heard Glenda say.

"Shift your weight backward. We'll be landing on a level surface," I said.

By the time I finished saying it, we already had.

9

I lurched slightly forward despite my stance, I heard the klaxon begin its warning and I hurled my grenade at the weapons bank.

I pushed Glenda against the far wall and shielded her from the explosion that followed. Before the echoes had died, I turned and dashed through the opening portal.

There was no one in sight. The klaxon kept wailing. I raced ahead.

Rounding the curved corridor's first big blind spot, I saw that the door to the Comp vault was still open. I swung around the massive metal frame and entered low, weapon extended.

But there was no need for such an entry. Only Gene and Jenkins were present, and I already knew that they were both dead. The manner of their passing was not especially important to me, though I noticed that Gene had been shot in the left temple and Jenkins had blood on his chest and abdomen. Faint memories of the attack came into my mind as I looked upon the scene. It is strange how a terminal mesh works. Had things been the other way around, they would know my final moments with a terrible clarity. It always seems to pass with more clarity from older members of the family to the younger, painfully enforcing a kind of seniority system in the descent of the nexus. Why this should be so, I do not know. Not that it really matters, I guess.

I crossed the room and killed the klaxon. Glenda entered as I was turning away from it, then halted and turned pale. I went to her, turned her about and pushed her back outside.

"This way," I said, and I led her on up the corridor.

The door to the Files vault was open also. I halted

when I saw this and proceeded toward it on my own. I edged close, went in quickly.

It was empty. But before I could relax, sigh, straighten, my eyes automatically moved to the most important part of the room, and there they remained.

Pins five, four, three and two had been pulled. The chair had been swiveled to the right. The helmet hung at a lopsided angle above it.

It was the ache in my shoulders that made me realize how tense my muscles had become. I took a deep breath, mopped my brow, turned.

For a little while, I refused to accept it. Whoever—whatever—he was inside, Black had added to it four of my own demons, three of whom I did not know. As one of the clones, there was no reason why he could not. But the thought that he might had not occurred to me, until then. Unprepared as I was, it came to me as a greater shock than anything that had happened recently, including my deaths and the disruption at Wing 5.

I leaned against the doorframe, keeping an eye on the corridor. Automatically, I found a cigarette and lit it. I had to think clearly and act very quickly now.

Locate him. That came first.

All right. He could be anywhere. He could still be around, or he could have returned to the House. The first thing, then, was to check with the Bandit, to see whether he had done anything recordable yet as Winkel. A negative there, and the second thing would be to commence searching Wing Null for him.

Dimly aware of Glenda's troubled presence, I returned to Comp. I did not note her reactions to the bodies this time, but she remained at my side.

But I did not query the Bandit. When I crossed over to it, my gaze was drawn downward to a red light that winked within the map of Wing Null that was laid beneath the clear surface of the countertop. It indicated that a hatch had been opened. If this was not a trick meant to distract me, then it meant that my quarry could have gone outside, onto the surface of the planet itself. The chronometer showed me that the hatch had only been opened about four minutes earlier.

"Damn him! What does he want?" I said, my mind racing.

142

Then I made my decision and seized Glenda by the hand.

"Come on! We are going back next door again. I have to show you something. It is urgent."

I took her back to the central console in Files. Fetching out my stiletto, I used it to chip away the blob of solder at the base of pin one. Then I turned to Glenda and realized that I was still holding her hand. Her eyes moved from the machinery to the blade to my face. I put the weapon away and lowered her hand, released it.

"I want to ask a favor," I said. "It is extremely important and I do not have time to explain what it represents."

"Go ahead and ask," she said.

"I am about to leave this place and go outside. I have no idea how long I will be out there, though I only intend it to be a brief while. When I return I might be confused, incoherent, injured. That would be the point at which I would need your assistance." I slapped the chair. "Should this occur, I want you to get me into this chair, even if you have to trank me to do it."

"With what?" she said.

"I'll give you a trank gun in a minute. If I seem in any way disturbed or—altered—get me into the chair and lower this hood over my head." I pushed it with my hand. "Then throw these switches—the entire row beginning at the left and taking them in order to the end. Everything else is properly set. Then all you have to do is wait until this blue light comes on. When that happens, pull this pin all the way out of the board. That's all."

"Then what happens?"

"I do not know—specifically, that is. But it is the only treatment I can think of for what might occur. I have to go now. Will you do it if it seems necessary—if I am dazed, bewildered?"

"Yes. If you will promise to answer my questions afterward."

"Fair enough. Please repeat the procedure back to me."

She did, and I hurried her outside once more.

"I will take you to a comfortable place near to the hatch," I said, "where you can wait, and view the surface outside. You will be able to see me depart and return."

I wondered about that light, though, and decided to

143

show her how to opaque the window if it became necessary.

". . . One other thing," I added. "I may not be me when I come back."

She halted.

"I beg your pardon," she said.

"My appearance could be different. Well, I could be another person."

"What you are saying then is that I force the next person I see under that machine, whether he likes the idea or not."

"Only if he seems confused, disturbed . . ."

"I'd think anybody would be if you tried to force him under that thing."

"It won't be just anybody. It will be me, in one form or another."

"All right. It will be done. But there is one other thing."

"What?"

"What if nobody comes back?"

"Then it is all over," I said. "Go home and forget all about this."

"How? I have no idea where we are, let alone how to get back."

"In the room of the dead men," I said, "low, and to the left of center on the far wall, there is a small green panel which controls the transport system. It is fairly simple. You would be able to figure it out if you had to."

I steered her into the lounge then, and she drew back against me, uttering a small cry. The window had been transpared. The moon was out of sight now, but a pale light suffused the landscape, indicating that the second moon—slower, larger, brighter—was already up, but blocked from our view for the moment.

"That is not just a picture. That is a real window, isn't it?" she said.

"Yes," I said, pushing her gently forward, passing around and fetching her a trank gun. "Do you know how to use one of these?"

She was advancing toward the window. She glanced at the gun, murmured, "Yes," and kept going, as if mesmerized. I crossed over, picked up her hand, placed it on her palm and closed her fingers over it.

"I have never seen the outside before—really," she said.

144

"Well, look all you want. I have to go now. There is a simple on-off switch to the left there, under the frame. That's right. That will opaque it for you, if you want."

"Why would I want to? It is beautiful."

"There is an optical phenomenon—a blinding light—which comes and goes. You will want to opaque it if it comes."

"Well, until that happens, I am just going to look. I—"

"Then goodbye for now. See you again soon."

"Wait!"

"I've waited too long already."

"But I saw something move out there. It could have been a man."

"Where?"

She pointed in the direction of the ruins.

"Over that way."

I did not see anything moving and she said, "Gone now," and I said, "Thanks," and left her standing there, looking out, wondering whether she was conscious of my departure.

I made my way on up the corridor to the recess that held the hatch. It was actually a series of three doors, offering various degrees of resistance and forms of protection. All three were undogged, and I passed through quickly, pausing only to check out the pistol.

It was cool, and the smells of the night came into my nostrils—damp, and tinged with the faint halations of growing things. In a moment, the feeling of novelty faded. I had been outside a few times before—long ago—and the impressions were not unfamiliar.

I quickly adjusted to movement across the irregular surface and struck off in the direction of the ruin. The silence was occasionally interrupted by little chirping noises, whether by bird or insect I could not tell. I passed through small pockets of fog whenever the ground dipped appreciably. The stones were moist and slippery. In clear spaces I had a shadow, so strong had the moonlight become. Turning, I could see the huge, white orb in its entirety, fat above my fortress now. A few wisps of cloud fled before it, but the sky was otherwise clear and blazing with countless stars. I was taken then by a series of peculiar feelings that began, I suppose, with something of doubt and apprehension.

145

The stellar panorama had something to do with it—those stars we had tried to make somehow obscene—as well as the still, stark landscape through which I moved, alone now for the first time in ages, outside the House, pursuing the most enigmatic individual of whom I had knowledge, in the direction of those puzzling ruins. It was unusual that I should think along these lines. The ruins had not been puzzling to me up until then. They were simply there, and that was it, a fact which also contributed to this odd moment's introspection. The possibility then occurred to me that peculiar things which did not normally strike me as puzzling were probably things about which I had once known something, and like a sword in a stone the edge of my curiosity was blunted at a subconscious level.

How many things had I known and forgotten? Would any of them be of value to me now? Was I rushing to my destruction by pursuing a man who knew almost everything that I knew, plus several lifetimes' experience of which I knew nothing? Possibly. But I thought I had this encounter worked out. The thing that bothered me was that he should be able to see it, too.

And why choose this place as our battlefield? It had to do with the ruins, I knew. I realized then that I was somewhat afraid of them. Why?

If only I had pulled more pins . . .

I moved ahead, ready for an ambush but doubting one would come, yet.

Not a sparkle, not a glimmer emerged from the ruins. They were still, their shadows only just now beginning to retreat from the moonlight.

My footfalls came soft, muffled. My breathing seemed the loudest thing about me . . .

The ground rose, then dipped again, and for a moment I had a very clear view for a good distance. He was nowhere in sight, though. There came a breeze, cool, light, and the fogs diminished, were gone, as I made my way onto higher ground.

I was aiming to kill a man in the name of pacificism, harmony, fraternity, and to maintain the integrity of the House. That his intentions toward me were also lethal was fairly obvious by now. While I was uncertain as to the principles involved, it was apparent that he disagreed with me on the question of cloistering humanity. This was sufficient reason to remove him, so far as I was concerned. However, while with anyone else I would simply have dismissed him as misguided, his persistence and occasional ingenuity had aroused my curiosity as to his reasons.

I had no doubts as to the correctness of my own beliefs, that human nature could be altered, that man could be forced to evolve morally. As I made my way about a small, scummy pool at the center of a crater, I did, for a moment, wonder why. It was not a questioning of the notions, simply a sudden curiosity as to where I had obtained them. It seemed that they had always been a part of my mental equipment. This being so, it struck me that with all those pulled pins Black and I now shared an ancestry with which he should be by far the more conversant. Such being the case, it would seem he should have acquired the proper philosophical attitude. There were several possibilities . . .

Either he possessed an overriding imperative to the contrary, he *had* been changed, or our early past was sufficiently ambiguous for him to live without altering his attitudes.

It may have been that all three were to some extent correct. The nature of the former was presently as unknowable to me as the ultimate source of my own sentiments. I mean, I was aware that my own notions were rational without necessarily being logical, that is to say, deductive. They were a part of my mental—"tradition" I guess is the best word. Say his feelings were as strong, and I suppose it was possible that the accumulations of four lifetimes dumped upon him by the pulling of the pins might not have swayed him over to my way of thinking. Still, there had to be some effect . . . It was like guessing at the results of a test wherein two virtually unknown chemicals were to be mixed and heated, though.

The third thought was what troubled me, as it touched on something of a sore spot I had but recently developed . . .

Namely, the possibility that my past was not so firm a thing as my present. Supposing there was actually something there to comfort and abet him? The reason for the partial suicide by means of the pin with each succession of

147

the nexus was more than personality adjustment for a permanent meshing. It was also intended as a progressively civilizing act, a further paring away on each occasion of those elements best classified as antisocial, in keeping with the evolving temper of the times. My present state of being was evidence of the effectiveness of the system. I was capable of things which I knew would have caused Lange or Engel to writhe, to recoil with revulsion, possibly to pass out. For the moment I was glad of this, because of the man I pursued. But although I felt myself a necessary evil, I regretted the necessity. The means were vindicated only because Black was an anachronism.

But what things lay behind the other pins? That was what troubled me. I knew what I had been until very recently, and I knew what I had become. The return had been a comfortable and natural thing, and I absorbed and dominated my later selves quite easily—as if they had been but brief moods. All the unsacrificed portions of Jordan were part of my memory; the rest I knew through the interface darkly when, at times of crisis, he became my personal demon. Offhand, I would say that he was a trifle meaner and more unprincipled than I. By extension, then, might not the even earlier versions of myself lend support rather than contradiction to whatever made Black run? I had been lifting myself by my own bootstraps, step by painful step. But what if I had not? What if there had been no overpowering will to improve my condition, and no effort? Black and I were of the same flesh. I did not understand how or why, but we were. And this was what made me apprehensive. The only real difference between us was an idea, or an ideal. And, as facets of the same person, we were still willing, in a completely literal sense, to kill ourself over it. The feeling that gripped me at that moment was not unlike the one that had taken Engel as he fled by ranks of jangling phones. Only I knew that if I answered, the voice on the other end would be my own.

Peering ahead, I picked my way among haphazard heaps of shattered stone. I contained my feelings, partly suppressed them, kept alert. He could be waiting in ambush at any point.

I passed a small crater within and about which the rocks had been fused. Almost immediately after that, the ground took a turn upward and I picked a broken course up the long incline, shards and splinters of some mineral glittering underfoot. Abruptly, I came to a high point beyond a stand of boulders, from which I could see the ruins about three-quarters of a mile distant.

I sought cover immediately and studied the prospect. It was still and clear in the moonlight, with no apparent movement anywhere, except for a few small flying things that dipped and darted quickly by. There was no light from within the ruins. I watched for a brief while, glanced back at the dark bulk of the Wing with its one small square of illumination, turned my eyes ahead once more.

Then I saw him.

Advancing quickly, he had just emerged from a jagged declivity that lay like a broken lightning bolt halfway across the plain. Dodging among rocks, he continued on toward the ruins.

I was after him immediately, racing down the slope, skidding and slipping, dislodging gravel. No need for stealth now I knew where he was. I broke into a run at the first opportunity. It appeared that he was indeed making his way toward that smashed fortress, and I felt a sudden need to reach him before he got there. I felt more troubled that he was heading for it than if he had been laying a simple ambush. His knowledge of the past being greater than mine, I feared that he knew to seek something within that might give him the edge in our coming conflict.

Down, then up again. There were no more major dips the rest of the way. It was all uphill, pocked, fused, cracked, strewn with rubble. Running became impossible before very long, but I pushed myself to my limits and gained on him. How long before he became aware of me?

Minutes later, it did not matter. I was closer to him than he was to the ruins. And the first couple of times he looked back he missed me somehow. I was gasping by then and very conscious of the rushing of blood in my temples. I slowed. I had to.

He caught sight of me shortly after that, stared a moment, turned and broke into a run. Cursing, I followed at the best pace I could manage. We were still too far apart to bother shooting at each other.

For a little while then, it was a question of hoping for him to tire quickly while I tried hard not to myself. If I

149

could just hold up a little longer, he might become convinced that this was the way it was going to work. I wanted him to decide that running was not going to get him where he was headed in time, so that he might as well turn and fight and get things over with, one way or the other.

He looked back again, and although it pained me I put on a burst of speed. We were almost within hailing distance. He faltered slightly, hurried again.

Slowly, things cleared a bit, steadied. It seemed my second wind was on its way. I began to feel that I would hold up. When he looked back about a minute later that was apparently his conclusion, too.

He veered to the right, making for an area of large stones and small rubble. Great! I did the same. I was not about to play it slow and careful when I was wearing body armor.

I had my pistol ready before he disappeared behind the nearest boulder. I swung wide as I passed it, but he was not there. He had kept going, and the first shot came at me from a stand of stone about a hundred feet away.

I held my own fire as I charged his position, waiting for him to show himself again, as he pulled back that first time. I was not going to waste a shot on that skimpy a target at that distance.

He did, at about fifty feet, and we both fired. I felt the impact on my chest armor, and my own shot ricocheted off the stone.

I kept running and we both kept firing. This time he did not retreat. My armor stopped two more of his shots, I believe. Then he jerked with one of mine. For a moment, my hopes rose.

We each got off one more shot, though.

It came as a blinding pain in the left side of my head, and I stumbled. My pistol fell from my numbed fingers.

I could not permit it to end that way. I thought that I heard a metallic click near to my head. Turning, I saw the tops of his shoes. My right arm was completely useless, but I could not let him simply stand there, reload and pull the trigger again.

I grabbed at his ankles with my left hand, and I caught one. The left, I think. He tried to pull free, but I was able to maintain my grip. Then he tried to kick me with his free foot, just as I jerked at his ankle and rolled myself toward him.

He went down.

I let go, and with my left hand I managed to get the bent stiletto out of my jacket.

It was too far to his heart or throat, though, and he was already moving again. The only thing I could see was to try severing the artery in his leg nearest me with the one slash I might be able to make. I might be able to throw myself on him and hold him down while he bled to death. Then only one ordeal would remain.

I made the thrust and he blocked it. He caught my wrist.

I tried to twist it away, but it was no use. He was hurt, weakened—I could even see the blood on his garments—but he still had the advantage. He brought his other hand across and began to pry my fingers loose from the weapon.

I was at the rearmost edge of consciousness by then, but even so I realized that this was it, that there was nothing left I could do.

He wrenched the blade free and reversed it. Ironic. My own weapon ... I had intended to kill him, block the mesh and so be rid of him forever. Now, though ...

The last thing that I saw before I felt the sting of the blade was his face. His expression was not one of triumph, however—only fatigue, and something of fear.

10

Silence, light, blood. Pain—
Too late. Too late . . .
Block . . . No! Through . . . Yes! Dizzy . . .
. . . And the light. The light!

I kept blinking. I kept blinking my eyes. I felt wet all over. Perspiration, blood, saliva . . .

My head was full of whirlwinds, catching thoughts, twisting them, juxtaposing images, driving my awareness in circles . . .

To stop thinking, to hold down my cerebration as much as possible, to confine my consciousness to the level of observing and reacting—this seemed the only way to maintain a measure of stability.

Pain. I hurt in many places, but the pain in my right hand was particularly intense. I had been staring at it all along, but now I forced my attention to cover this area of existence.

My hand had grown white from the strain of gripping the hilt of the blade which protruded from the throat of the man lying across my legs. There was a bullet wound above his left eye, and blood on his forehead and cheek as well as his neck.

Yes, yes, I understood, but I pushed that out of my mind as soon as it occurred and considered the problem of my hand. I squeezed it and tugged at my fingers, bringing back another memory I immediately suppressed. Gradually, they relaxed, and I cried out involuntarily at the untying of the knots in my muscles. Once free, though, I let the hand fall immediately and squeezed my eyes tightly shut.

The light—
It hurt, directed as the beam was, full in my face. I turned my head away, opened my eyes again. It was still

too bright, off to the side now. I decided to go away from it. For that matter, I wanted to get away from the corpse, too.

Slowly, I pulled myself free, keeping my head averted from the body and the light. I immediately became very aware of my other pains, particularly the moist area at my waist, on the right side. I got to my feet, though, and leaned back against the boulder beside which I had lain, breathing heavily and dizzy again for several moments.

I felt as if I stood in the middle of a nightmare, afraid to think of what had just happened, afraid of what might be coming. As soon as the world stood still, I pushed myself forward and began walking. I followed the big white moon downhill.

. . . To get away from that blazing light. But it followed me.

I veered to the right, then to the left. I quickened my pace. It remained with me, though.

I fought back a flash of frenzy.

"No! Don't think! For God's sake, don't think!" I said aloud, surprising myself with my own voice.

Don't think. That way lay panic, confusion, chaos. Entertain only one notion at a time and concentrate on it to the exclusion of all else.

I fixed my attention on my movements, counting my steps, staring at my surroundings, thinking about my feet, my legs.

But I was going in the wrong direction.

Wasn't I?

Yes.

Yes, I was supposed to be heading toward the ruin. I—

"Don't think!" I reminded myself. "Get away! Get away!"

Yes. It was more important that I get away from that light than do anything else just then. Good thought. Hold that.

But—

Hold it! Get away!

I moved quickly. Fifty paces. A hundred. Go right. Fifty paces. Angle left. Fifty . . .

The brightness followed, casting my changing shadows far before me, illuminating my way. It was an eerie thing to behold, and I ran, seeking some barrier that could be interposed between myself and the source of the light.

I saw a suitable formation a few hundred yards away and raced toward it, moved around to its far side, rested there panting. Automatically, I reached for a cigarette.

Cigarette? There were none. But that was right. Winkel did not smoke. Rather— Wait! Black— No!

Don't think. I chewed my lip. The light could not reach me. It was dark, and I was alone in a quiet place. I sighed. I tried to relax, and felt my breathing begin to slow. My heartbeat followed its example. The throbbing pain in my side changed to a dull ache. It still bled, though not so profusely. I kept the palm of my hand pressed against it.

I had to go back, to get to the ruin. But that damned light— If it would just go out, I could be on my way.

But why? Why the ruin? What I really wanted was to get away and— No! Wait! Wait . . .

I had destroyed the last of them. It was all over now.

No.

I had finally gotten Mr. Black.

No.

No?

No!

Then Hell's lid was lifted. I/he had been too weak to resist the final meshing. The most horrible result of this realization was a desire to laugh and to scream simultaneously. Realizing what had occurred was not tantamount to accepting it—or being able to do anything about it. Helplessly, I regarded what I had become: namely, literally, looking at it from both directions at once, I was my own worst enemy. I believe I did laugh, or snort, momentarily. I was haled through corridors of memory where all the actions recalled were driven by sentiments and desires which now encountered their opposites at every hand. I began to choke. It was too much. Much too much. It was pulling me apart.

I was completely unable to help myself at that point. Whatever I thought or felt, there came an immediate reaction, a countersurge of guilt, anger, fear. The thing that saved me, that slammed the lid on all of this once more, came from the only place that it could—the outside world. I was distracted.

It was a noise, not loud and quite distant, but completely out of place. Metallic. Recurrent.

Suddenly, my existence was concentrated in my senses, and the residue of the past moments' emotions consolidated into an overall wariness.

I listened, moved to my right, dropped low, peered around the edge of my rocky shield. The light still bathed the other side of the stone, though for a moment or so it did not shine directly into my eyes. It did catch me more squarely very soon after that, as it played back and forth upon the stone, but not before I had caught sight of the source of the noise.

It was a squat robot of some sort, with four cablelike extensors and photoelectric eyes, rolling toward my position on dark treads.

I turned immediately and raced away. That it was coming for me, I had no doubt.

Down. Then up. Then down again. The light followed for a time, but the angle of the slope quickly took me below its reach. I slowed, puffing, pressing my hand to my side. I had to ration my energies carefully. The fact that much of the remaining course was downhill would be of help.

I looked back, but the machine was out of sight beyond the ridge. Ahead, the moon silvered the face of the fortress of Wing Null. I could make out the solitary, lighted window. I could trace the trails I had followed. The ground-clinging mists, the pockets of fogs, of vapors, were touched with phosphorescence. The moist rocks glistened like black glass. I felt that I had an even chance of making it ahead of my mechanical pursuer.

I could still hear the thing periodically, scattering pebbles, scraping stones, coming along my trail at a good clip. Whether, ultimately, I would owe it thanks or blame, I did not know. While I had been tormented by that light, I had also been attracted by it. Now that I knew, to some extent, who I was, it made understanding a little easier. We really had been trying to reach the ruins—just why, I was uncertain. It was not just part of an elaborate ploy to get the last of them/us. No. And the desire to go there was still strong within me. That light was several things, I felt, and one of them was a beacon, a call, to me. Only the me that it reached was no longer the me for whom it had been intended. Part of me had been startled by it, frightened, had drawn away. Its call persisted, however, and even as I fled I had been attracted by the summons. This ambivalence was resolved in favor of continued flight, though, with the appearance of the robot. There had to be some sort of intelligence behind the thing. Not understanding what it represented was sufficient reason to flee it.

It was not very long, though, before the sounds grew louder. The thing seemed to be moving faster now. I kept glancing back as I went.

I dodged among jagged stone formations, rifts, ravines, craters, getting down near to the misted area once more. I had small hope of losing the robot there, however, as I realized that the level attitude of the area would soon see me back within range of that light. Staring then, I thought I caught glimpses of it sweeping the prospect far ahead.

Forcing myself to hurry, I stumbled, almost panicked at my slowness in regaining my feet, pulled myself together, proceeded more deliberately.

The robot continued to pick up speed, was moving faster than I was moving. It was not precise and undeviating in its course, however, as it did take blind turns, halt, back up, alter direction, circle objects. Seeing this, I dodged behind a rock and altered my course to keep as many obstructions as possible between myself and the thing. Still, it seemed cognizant of my general direction. I began to have second thoughts concerning my ability to outdistance it once I was out in the open and on level ground. What the devil was I to do?

Knock it blind, you fool!

The jolt lasted only a moment, for it was but a part of me that was unfamiliar with my demons.

"How?" I asked.

Turn your head farther to the right. —Stop! See that scarp? Get to it and climb it!

"I will be spotted."

That is the idea. Go!

I went. He had a plan, which was more than I did. If you can't trust your demon, whom can you trust?

The idea splashed in as I moved toward the escarpment. Nothing very complicated about it—which, considering the circumstances, was good.

The sounds of increased activity upslope warned me

156

that I had been detected. When I looked back, the machine was racing toward me. I quickened my pace, and when I looked ahead again I realized what a steep slope it was that lay before me.

I began to climb immediately, however, not even bothering to look back.

Thus doth fear make athletes of us all.

"You're right," I said, my blood pounding, the sounds of pursuit coming louder.

I wondered as I went whether the thing would essay this slope or just try to wait me out. I did not believe that it could make it all the way to the top, because I was not even certain that I could. It kept steepening, and I had to seek handholds as well as footholds, finally. My grip was weak, and my side kept aching and oozing. When I achieved a height where I felt safe from the machine my greatest fear came to be that I would pass out and fall.

Gasping, I was able to pull myself up onto the broad shelf we had spied, about forty-five feet above the ground, where I collapsed. I believe that I was unconscious then for a brief while.

It was the sounds from below that aroused me. But not quickly. My limbs felt weighted, my head ready to explode. Tag ends of thoughts and images, like bits of dream, coalesced and fell away before I could scrutinize them closely.

I propped myself on my elbows, raised my head and turned to look over the edge and down.

The robot was attempting to mount the slope. It had attained a height of about fifteen feet. The angle of the incline increased at that point, and it was grinding its way very slowly, forward and upward, its extensors flailing after rocky projections.

Get to it! Get to it!

"All right! Damn it!" I muttered. "All right!"

I cast about, looking for ammunition. Most of the stones seemed either too large or too small. I cataloged them quickly. Should I try to roll down a big one or hurl some of the smaller stones? My muscles answered that one.

I got to my knees, then rose, collected a dozen or so of the fist-sized ones into a heap near the edge. By then the machine had advanced another yard and had succeeded in catching hold of a solid projection. It continued its advance.

I threw three of the stones. Two missed completely and one struck the chassis, low. Double damn! I threw two more, and only one passed near the receptors.

It found another hold, drew itself four or five feet nearer, reached forward again.

My next rock smashed a receptor. It was a lucky cast, but it raised my hopes. I bounced all my remaining stones off its chassis, though, without noticeable effect.

By then it was around twenty-five feet up and still moving. Its angle seemed quite precarious, but its whiplike appendages were of a heavy, shiny cable that looked more than adequate to support it so.

I sought out more ammunition. I located a cabbage-sized stone which I pitched at it underhanded, using both hands.

It crashed against the robot with considerable force. To my surprise, the thing halted for several moments, just hanging there. Slowly, however, it resumed its upward course.

I struggled with another rock, about three times the size of the previous one, and managed to repeat the performance. This time the machine emitted a brief burst of clicking noises before it began to move again.

But I had just about depleted my arsenal. Of readily manageable stones, that is. There were some that were quite sizable, but I all but despaired of moving one. However . . .

There was one farther back and somewhat higher up. Certainly large enough to produce the havoc I desired. If I could dislodge it, it would roll. If it would roll, it might make it to the edge and over. If it did that and went over at the right spot, my immediate worries would be over.

. . . Unfortunately, it was irregularly shaped, and I could not be certain as to the precise course it would follow.

As I stood there thinking about it, the robot suddenly jerked forward another three or four feet and immediately began casting upward after anchoring positions. I turned hurriedly and headed for the stone. The machine had already passed the halfway mark.

At first, I was unable to budge it. I must have thrown

my full weight against it six or eight times before it moved slightly. By then, my arms felt almost useless and the combination of my headache and dizziness with the pain in my side were about to prostrate me. But the fact that it had moved at all strengthened me a little more. I shoved twice again and it stirred on both occasions. By then the sounds of the robot were frighteningly near.

I tried bracing my back against the slant of the shelf and pushing with my legs. It increased the pain in my side, but it moved it some more. Turning my head, I saw the extensors whipping up over the edge of my aerie, seeking holds, falling back, coming again. I renewed my efforts.

The stone shuddered, swayed forward, rocked back. Again.

Again.

It almost toppled. But I felt drained. Unable to push another time. Hardly able to move . . .

Two of the extensors caught onto something. A labored humming sound followed, to be joined moments later by a screeching from the treads. But I still had not recovered my strength. I lay there aching and hearing.

There came a glint of light, another as it backtracked and overshot, and then the beam was upon me once again. Cursing, I turned my head away. In that instant, I found the extra strength that I needed.

I tensed my legs, almost convulsively, and began to push. My teeth were clenched so tightly I thought they would all crack. Fresh perspiration broke out upon my brow and ran into my eyes. My side throbbed in time with my heart.

Then, slowly, slowly, the stone moved forward. It moved several inches, I would judge, before it stuck. I relaxed and let it rock back. Then I tensed again and shoved.

This time it kept going beyond the point where it had halted before. It slowed but kept moving, and I continued the pressure until I thought that I would explode.

It slowed, began to bind, felt as if it were about to stop. Then it went forward and I went supine.

I would have missed seeing what happened next except for the fact that my head rolled to the left and the light struck me in the eyes again. I twisted away and by that movement obtained a view of the stone's progress.

The forward section of the robot was in sight—ten or twelve inches' worth. The stone seemed to be going wide, and I feared that it might miss.

But it did not. It caught the left corner of the thing with a magnificent crash. Then both were gone. I heard the sounds of its impact below just as I was passing out again.

Just how long I lay there then, I do not know. I think that I dreamed, of stars, without number, drifting like bright isles in a dark lake, of men, going to and fro among them, peaceful, serene, wise, noble. I seemed to be pleased by this, for conflicting reasons: either the work I had set out to accomplish had been finished, and finished properly, or this had occurred in spite of what had been done, and because of its speedy termination. Either way, it was a pretty, if unframed, picture and I regretted being drawn away from it. I guess it was the light that roused me. When I finally came around, I could not be certain whether I had actually been dreaming or simply staring up at the stars in a kind of reverie. Not that it really mattered.

I turned over and managed to get onto my hands and knees, keeping my face averted from the light. Slowly, I crawled to the edge.

The robot lay, broken, twisted, on its back, all the way down and perhaps thirty feet out. The stone was nowhere in sight.

I lowered myself to my stomach and lay there staring at it, feeling at first elated, then depressed. What was I but some sort of broken mechanism myself? Preserving only what I deemed essential, I had streamlined myself at each accession, wound me up and run until I stopped. Then again.

Or, rather, he had.

Damn it! No! *I* had.

We had?

All right. I was beginning to accept what had occurred. Things had been sorting themselves out unconsciously ever since that most recent meshing. All of the pin-pulling, with its resultant restoration of memories I had previously stripped away, produced psychic shocks of varying intensity, but the material revealed was ultimately assimilable because it was mine, it was familiar, it had fit and

160

belonged. Then came the alien nexus, through which other portions of my original self had been filtered.

Alien, though? Not any longer.

No.

For, in an instant, I was on the other side of the mirror, regarding the detestable baggage I had acquired by the pulling of the pins and the killing of Winton. Even so, I had not obtained what I wanted—an understanding of the ultimate motivation of that gang of meddlers.

Meddlers? I was, too, of course. But it was in reaction to them.

Them?

Us. Now.

Funny.

. . . For none of us knew why we kept winding ourselves up in a certain way—whichever the way—or who we really were. I had indeed been the missing clone, a theft made necessary at that time by virtue of my advanced age and declining powers. It had taken a carefully controlled suicide to effect the transfer without allowing the others to become aware of my true nature. Before that, I had been around for generations, almost from the beginning. But there things grew murky. I had always known that I was of one blood with the enemy; and we had always been enemies, for I had disagreed from the first with their dispositions in the setting up of the House. I had been powerless, though, and had bided my time, disapproving. I knew them both from their actions and as an occasional silent party to their meshings. It was a long while before my distrust of their policy of confinement and progressive control reached the point where I began to consider their removal.

The House had only been intended as a temporary measure—the linking and consolidation of all the outposts as a common shelter for humanity following the disaster that had engulfed the Earth—a place to pause for a second breath, as it were. The family had decided to make it more permanent, however, holding that the same thing would happen again, wherever we went, unless something was done to change man himself. They were for making the human race a prisoner and a patient, as I saw it. My own feelings were that simple dispersal would be sufficient to guarantee human continuity, by virtue of divergence,

161

divergence and the multiplicity of opportunities for development that would lie available. I had been back to Earth in its last days, working with the evacuation teams, and I believed it had all been an accident, a misunderstanding, a mistake, the war, the disaster. And even if this were not so, the same thing need not occur over and over again. I wanted man out of the House and on his way once more.

I lacked the organization and capability of the family. All that I shared was the anonymity. I decided to take advantage of it to the fullest and plan carefully, strike quickly and be thorough. I failed the first time, but they still did not know who or why it was. The authorities were useless, unaware of the family's existence and subject to its influence. I studied their methods, emulated them in concealing myself and, yes, learned something of their early ruthlessness. It was not that difficult.

They changed, though. I knew why. That notion of moral evolution they entertained and practiced, even on a personal level. That finally undid them. This time they were too weak and I had won—in a Pyrrhic sort of way.

I did not know who I really was either. My earliest memories involved wandering in the Cellar of Wing 1, where I eventually came to work, for a time, as a maintenance man. It was only gradually, by observation and telepathy, that I learned of the family and their grand experiment. I resolved to thwart them and I set out to educate myself.

I knew that by destroying them I might be throwing away the key to my own origin. I was willing to make this sacrifice, however . . .

The pins I was able to pull did not bring me this knowledge. If I had responded to the light sooner, I might have . . .

What was it about that light? As soon as it fell upon me back in the lounge I had been drawn to it. If I had not paused to seek knowledge of the pins, I would have reached it. I would have avoided . . .

No good.

I would have avoided a conflict that was really necessary for the successful completion of my work. Now it was just a matter of maintaining stability, of keeping the upper hand within my own being. I . . .

But I no longer wanted to follow the light. Now I was repelled by it. I—

We . . .

Yes. We.

No. I.

We are I.

I stared at the broken machine, sharing its wreckage.

Time ticked by.

The light spilled over my head from the back, casting me in Rorschachs of shadow.

My head continued to throb.

A small breeze herded sheep of mist past the robot.

Something dark and quick darted through the air.

Something tiny and not too near croaked and buzzed, briefly.

In the corner of my seeing, the moon was a wheel of ice, rolling.

My teeth began to chatter. My fingertips felt icy where they touched against the stone.

Get up!

"I—"

You have to climb down now and go back. Get up.

"I am tired."

Get up. Now.

"I don't know whether I can."

You can. Get up.

"I don't know whether I want to."

What you want is immaterial. Get up.

"Why?"

Because I said so. Now!

"All right! All right!"

I pushed myself up, slowly. I rested a moment on my hands and knees, then sat back on my haunches.

"Better?"

Yes. Now stand up.

I did. After a few seconds' vertigo had passed, I knew that I could hold it. I kept my back to the light, which had me facing Wing Null.

That is where you are headed. Get going.

I lowered my head, took several deep breaths and set about it.

Climbing down, I discovered, was not as difficult as

163

climbing up. Especially when I slipped and slid the last eight feet or so.

Rise. Go on. Go on.

"Am I never to rest?" I asked. But I found my footing once more and began to walk, bent partly forward, clutching my side. My descent had put me out of range of the light again, and that helped some. I passed the robot without granting it a second look. I climbed, I descended, I staggered. I stumbled and rose again, went on.

The exertion warmed me somewhat. After a time, I sighted the dark bulk of my Wing once more. The lighted window reminded me of Glenda, which in turn made me think of her father. He had been my friend, and I had destroyed him. Not the same I. Not then. Not now. I tried to regard it in this fashion and felt the beginnings of acceptance. It was not that I was beyond remorse, but that I was no longer the same person I had been—then, or even a few days or hours earlier. Perhaps the shattering and restructuring of my ego was less debilitating than it might have been because I had had so much practice at it. I understood now who I had been—up to a point. That was a beginning, anyway, of finding out who I was currently.

I had encouraged Glynn, seeing in him a hope for the future, a means of breaking out of the House. I had come to like him personally, however, and when they destroyed him I had taken the child. I had had no special plans for her then. I had done it solely because of my friendship with her father. Later, though, when I saw that her intellectual endowments were quite formidable, I saw to it that along with an extensive education she was also aware of her father's hopes and plans, down to the level of details. She embraced them with enthusiasm. By then though, I had almost come to consider her more mine than his. So it was only natural that I eventually made her privy to some of my own hopes and plans as well. She was completely sympathetic, which is why I had enlisted her aid. I wished now that I could have done without her. She did not know I was going to kill Engel or force Winton to kill me. Still, it had worked. I could see no other way. I had won . . .

But it had worked and I had won, then why was I headed for Wing Null rather than the ruin?

Because . . .

Keep walking.

There had to be a reason. I just could not recall it. My head was as foggy as the night about me. It still throbbed like a sore tooth.

Do not try to think. Just keep walking.

Glenda. That was it. She was waiting for me. I was going back to see Glenda, to tell her it was all over now.

Get up!

Strange. I did not remember having fallen. I struggled to my feet and almost immediately collapsed again.

It is not very much farther. You must continue. Get up.

I wanted to. I wanted to cooperate. This spirit was quite willing . . .

. . . Only my legs kept getting tangled, doing the wrong things. Damned uncooperative, this body . . .

Pendulumlike, I could feel my mind doing strange things again, too. It was all right, though, if it would just make me go.

Another try, then down again.

A little thing like that should not bother me, though. It was not necessary that I stand in order to proceed. I had driven bodies beyond this point before. It was all a matter of attitude. Singlemindedness, determination—these were what mattered. Perhaps stubbornness was a better word.

I crawled forward. Time ceased to have meaning. My hands were cold.

Up a slope. I hardly noticed when the light hit me again after a time. When I did realize it, it brought me the passing illusion of being onstage, performing before an invisible audience, utterly silent, so taken were they by my performance.

Just before my arms gave way for the third time, I saw the Wing again, I saw the window.

It was near now, much nearer. Slowly, very slowly, I pulled myself along, like a half-crushed insect. It would be ridiculous to fail at this point. Absurd . . .

It was an effort to open my eyes partway and raise my head. How long had I been lying there?

No good.

One can lash the body, drive it, push it. But the comings and goings of the mind follow a different set of rules.

This one was a going. . . .

165

Part III

Of course, when the alternatives to certainty have
been exhausted and a negative answer remains all we
re [illegible] the unproven — then the [illegible]
measure of boredom is needed, though [illegible]

From a timeless vantage, I saw it all.

The family had picked me up, loaded me and pointed me at Styler. Styler had taken me, manipulating circumstances in a pattern that programmed me to play Othello to his Hamlet, and turned me loose to condition humanity along pacifistic lines he deemed propitious. I could only guess, but it seemed fairly obvious that he had obtained a specimen of my tissues at some point in my early experiments with cloning. He had robots capable of managing that much for him—still had robots—and he had designed Wing Null. The means was not really that material. Somewhere, he had used that sample to clone the original Mr. Black, implanted suggestions that made him something of an anti-me and sent him into the House with amnesia and his survival instinct going for him. He was placed there to check me and balance my efforts when the time came, operating like some sort of sociological time bomb. The time had come and this had happened. A wall was down, Glenda was ready with the Glynn formulations and I had been neutralized. I could almost hear Styler's voice saying, ". . . Now add 8 cc's of Black base to the di Negri acid."

I glared back at the colored lights. Finally, I reached out and began throwing switches.

I heard a startled noise from my right and a hand came forward and fell upon my arm. I could not turn my head to see her because of the hood. I had a vision from long ago of peasants plowing a small field, its boundary marked by an animal skull mounted on a low post.

"It's all right," I said.

The hand slipped away.

"Who—?" she finally said.

How the hell was I supposed to answer that?

"I was Legion," I said finally, haltingly, "a whole gallery of faces. I was Black, I was Engel, I was Lange, I was Winton, I was Karab, I was Winkel. And Jordan and Hinkley and Old Lange. And a horde of others of whom you have never heard. I should say that it does not matter, but it does, for I am me. I suppose that I should choose a face. Very well. Just call me Angelo. That is how it all began."

"I am afraid that I do not understand. Are you—?"

I raised the hood from my head and turned to regard her.

"Yes," I said, "I am really all right. Thank you for doing as I asked. Did I make it all the way back, or did you have to drag me?"

"I helped," she said. "I saw you fall."

"You mean you went outside?"

Her face brightened.

"Yes. I was hoping for an excuse. Not that kind, I mean. But—it was so fine!"

I rubbed my side.

"You patched me up some, I see."

"You were bleeding."

"Yes, I guess I was, wasn't I?"

I got to my feet, steadied myself for a moment against the back of the chair, moved to the counter and began searching the shelf beneath it.

"What are you looking for?"

"Cigarettes. I want to smoke."

"There were some in the other room, where I was waiting."

"Let's go there then."

I refused her arm. We walked into the hallway and up it.

"How long since you brought me in?" I asked.

"About an hour and a quarter."

I nodded.

"What has that light been doing recently?"

"I don't know. I haven't looked since I brought you in."

We came to the room, entered it. She indicated the cigarettes, declined one herself. I moved to the window and looked out as I lit up. A puddle of tawny light, spilled at the far edge of things, was seeping across the sky. I inhaled deeply, sighed smoke.

170

"You really liked it out there?" I said.

"Yes—and it is so beautiful now, with the sun starting to come up."

"Good. I want you to come take a walk with me outside."

"You're not in such great shape."

"All the more reason to have someone with me then. Besides, I'll need a secretary."

She cocked her head to one side and narrowed her eyes. I smiled.

"Come on. We'll take it slow and easy. The walk will do us good."

She nodded and followed me out to the locks. We passed through them and entered the cool morning.

"I can't get over the smells," she said, drawing a deep breath. "The air is so different from that in the House!" Then, "Where are we going?" she asked.

I turned my head and raised it.

"Up there."

"To the ruin? That is pretty far . . ."

"Slow and easy. No hurry," I said. "We have all the time in the world."

We started in that direction, and I was irritated by my need to stop and rest frequently. We had to go out of our way, also, for I directed our course in such a fashion that we did not pass near to the body I had left. Although I tried to conceal the pull in my side, she noted it and moved around and took my arm. This time I allowed it.

I chuckled.

"Remember when I gave you those skates for your seventh birthday?" I said. "And you slipped and twisted your ankle the very next day? I thought it was sprained, but it was really broken. You wouldn't let me carry you, though. You leaned on me like this. You didn't want to cry, but your face was all wet and you kept biting your lip. You tore that little blue dress you liked so much when you fell. The one with the yellow stitching on the front."

Her fingers had tightened to an almost painful grip upon my arm. A light breeze came out of the east. I reached over and patted her hand, "It *is* all right now," I said, and she nodded quickly and I turned away.

Before I saw it, I felt the glint from that light in the ruins. It flickered by, returned, stayed with us. It was not quite so overpowering when the air was filling with daylight.

We worked our way among the stones, about the craters, up the hill, down, then up again.

"A bird!" she cried.

"Yes. Pretty. Yellow."

It was a pleasant morning that was being fetched into the world, softening the tones of the landscape where my nightmare had been enacted. Some piled cumulus to the left promised a later rain, as did a cool breeze from that direction, but the east was still clear in its brightening and there was more greenery about than I had thought.

The light he had used to hunt me was finally blocked by the upper edge of that portion of the building's front which still stood, blackened and cracked, doors gaping, as we approached.

"Are we going in there?" she asked.

"Yes."

We moved forward and entered the caved-in, burnt-out lobby, skylighted by the collapsed roof, filled with the detritus of centuries.

"What are we going to do here?" she asked, as we picked our way through the litter in the direction of the more sheltered southwest corner of the room.

"In a minute. I think you will know in a minute or so," I said. "That's why I wanted a secretary."

The rear hallway I had taken so many years before was completely blocked by a cave-in that appeared to have been augmented by a landslide from the high hills to the rear. I led her into a relatively clear waiting alcove where the shapes of furniture persisted within piles of dust. Yes, I had remembered correctly. The dark instrument crouched, tarantula-like, in its recess in the wall. I withdrew my handkerchief.

While I was wiping it off, the telephone rang.

Glenda uttered a brief, incoherent noise that might have been part question.

"There," I said, stepping back, "I have it reasonably clean now. Answer the phone for me, will you?"

She nodded, and with a mixture of great puzzlement and some trepidation, moved forward and lifted the receiver.

"—Hello?"

172

She listened a moment, then covered the mouthpiece and looked at me.

"He wants to know who I am."

"So tell him," I said.

She did, listened again, covered it and sought me once more.

"He wants to know if Mr. Angelo di Negri is here."

"You are Mr. Negri's secretary. Ask him what he wants."

Again, and, "He wants to talk to you about your work," she said.

"I am busy just now," I said, as I began dusting a chair. "Tell him that you will fill him in a bit and describe to him the structure of the House, with its Wing setup and its internal organization. Answer any questions he has about it."

This took a long while. I had finished cleaning the filth of ages from the chair, doing a very thorough job, and had seated myself in it before she turned to me again.

"He wants to know whether he can speak with you now."

I shook my head. I lit a cigarette.

"Tell him that the wall is down on Wing V, and that people are going outside. Tell him that you are going back to provide a program for sheltering the exodus that is to come."

"I am?"

"You want to, don't you?"

"Yes, but—"

"You possess knowledge of the necessary equipment? Of its fabrication and employment?"

"I think so."

"Then tell him about that, too."

I finished smoking. After a long while, I lit another one.

"He wants to know what you think has been learned from all this," she said finally.

"How the hell should I know?" I said. "I am not even certain what I have learned myself, except that I now appreciate what it feels like to have been assumed into the workings of a great machine."

She spoke with him briefly, then said, "He says he would like to hear your voice. He says he would like you to say something to him. Anything."

173

I rose to my feet and stretched.

"Tell him the debt of honer is canceled between us," I said. "Tell him you are sorry, but Mr. Negri is not receiving any calls at this time. Then hang up."

She did this, and I accepted her arm once more and allowed her to help me back out of the ruin. The sun was up and the clouds were nearer. I thought we might be able to beat the rain. Then again, maybe not, but what the hell.

Other SIGNET Science Fiction You Will Enjoy

☐ **LEVEL 7 by Mordecai Roshwald.** A horrifying prophetic document of the future—the diary of a man living 4000 feet underground in a society bent on atomic self-destruction. (#T5011—75¢)

☐ **CLARION An Anthology of Speculative Fiction and Criticism from the Clarion Writers' Workshop edited by Robin Scott Wilson.** The Clarion Workshop is the only writers' program dealing with speculative fiction. The alumni represent twenty states and from this workshop many fresh and important voices will emerge to set the tone and influence the direction of science fiction in the seventies. Included are **Fritz Leiber** and **Samuel Delaney.** (#Q4664—95¢)

☐ **THE WORLD INSIDE by Robert Silverberg.** An unflinching look into a future as frightening as it is chillingly believable. It is the time of Urbmon, unlimited procreation and group identity. "One of the most fascinating and ingenious science fiction novels to appear in years." —**The Science Fiction Book Club** (#Q5176—95¢)

☐ **A CIRCUS OF HELLS by Poul Anderson.** The story of a lost treasure guarded by curious monsters, of captivity in a wilderness, of a journey through reefs and shoals that could wreck a ship, and of the rivalry of empires. (#T4250—75¢)

Other SIGNET Science Fiction Titles You Will Enjoy

☐ **GREYBEARD by Brian Aldiss.** Science fiction with a difference about an almost desolate future in which mankind and mammals have been rendered sterile by a cosmic "accident." (#Q5141—95¢)

☐ **DOWNWARD TO THE EARTH by Robert Silverberg.** Earthman Edmund Gundersen gambles his body and soul in an alien game where the stakes are immortality. (#T4497—75¢)

☐ **THE DEMOLISHED MAN by Alfred Bester.** A science fiction tale of a ruthless killer who pits his resources against infallible mind-reading detectives. (#T4461—75¢)

☐ **ISLANDS IN THE SKY by Arthur C. Clarke.** An engrossing novel of a future Earth encircled by terrifyingly dangerous manned satellites. (#Q5521—95¢)

☐ **TOMORROW I A Science Fiction Anthology edited by Robert Hoskins.** Five fascinating speculations on tomorrow featuring **Poul Anderson, John D. MacDonald, James H. Schmitz, Clifford D. Simak** and **William Tenn.** (#T4663—75¢)

THE NEW AMERICAN LIBRARY, INC.,
P.O. Box 999, Bergenfield, New Jersey 07621

Please send me the SIGNET BOOKS I have checked above. I am enclosing $_____(check or money order—no currency or C.O.D.'s). Please include the list price plus 25¢ a copy to cover handling and mailing costs. (Prices and numbers are subject to change without notice.)

Name_____

Address_____

City_____State_____Zip Code_____
Allow at least 3 weeks for delivery